PUFFIN BOOKS

THE GREAT DREAM ROBBERY

THE GREAT DREAM ROBBERY

GREG JAMES AND CHRIS SMITH

Illustrations by Amy Nguyen

PUFFIN

PUFFIN BOOKS

UK | USA | Canada | Ireland | Australia
India | New Zealand | South Africa

Puffin Books is part of the Penguin Random House group of companies
whose addresses can be found at global.penguinrandomhouse.com.

www.penguin.co.uk   www.puffin.co.uk   www.ladybird.co.uk

Penguin
Random House
UK

First published 2021
001

Text copyright © Greg James and Chris Smith, 2021
Illustrations copyright © Amy Nguyen, 2021

The moral right of the authors and illustrator has been asserted

Set in Baskerville MT Pro
Text design by Mandy Norman
Printed in Great Britain by Clays Ltd, Elcograf S.p.A

The authorized representative in the EEA is Penguin Random House Ireland,
Morrison Chambers, 32 Nassau Street, Dublin D02 YH68

A CIP catalogue record for this book is available from the British Library

ISBN: 978–0–241–47051–0
International paperback ISBN: 978–0–241–47050–3

All correspondence to:
Puffin Books
Penguin Random House Children's
One Embassy Gardens, 8 Viaduct Gardens, London SW11 7BW

To all the teachers who keep everyone reading and dreaming

CONTENTS

Are you ready for an adventure beyond your **wildest dreams**? You are? Alright, hold on a minute. You need to meet the characters first!

MAYA CLAYTON

TEDDY FLAMEWOOD

BEA FLAMEWOOD

PROFESSOR DEXTER

LILITH DELAMERE

GENERAL PHEARE

JULIA FLAMEWOOD

MATT FLAMEWOOD

BIN BAG THE CAT

CHAPTER 1
THE STRANGER
IN THE DREAM

'Ten minutes! Come on, please, just another ten minutes!'

'No!'

'Oh . . . *please*! All right, then – five minutes. Just five more minutes!'

'No, I told you already. It's bedtime! There's school tomorrow.'

'Yeah, but there aren't any really important lessons. Not in the morning anyway. Go on . . . just another five minutes. **Pleeeeeeeeeease?**'

'Mum . . . no! I really need to get to bed.'

'Oh, come on, Maya. You can sit up with me for another five minutes, surely?'

Maya Clayton stopped at the bottom of the stairs and huffed with frustration. Behind her, her mum sat cross-legged on the sofa cradling a mug of hot chocolate in both hands. Maya hesitated – it all looked very warm and inviting. But Maya had two very particular reasons why she didn't want to sit up chatting to her mum.

The first reason was an invisible force field of sadness that made the room much less inviting than it seemed at first glance. Looking past her mum, Maya could visualize it quite clearly, stirring the air like a chilly draught. It radiated out from an empty armchair next to the sofa. It was the chair where her father – Professor Dexter Clayton – would normally have been sitting, until the terrible accident six weeks ago.

The second reason why Maya Clayton was desperate to get to bed is harder to explain but all the more interesting for it. For dramatic reasons, we're not going to tell you about it until later in the chapter, but it's worth waiting for, we promise.

Maya's eyes lingered on the vacant chair and her mum followed her gaze. 'He'll be back sitting there before you know it,' she promised, though it was hard to tell who she was trying to convince. 'I know you miss him. Come on, come and sit with me for a bit. It might help to talk about it, you know.'

Maya – who had taken a tentative step back into the room – hesitated. She didn't want to talk. How could she possibly express all the things she was feeling right now? Some things are just too sad for words to do them justice.

Seeing her expression change, her mum back-pedalled: 'OK, OK! No talking necessary. Look, we can just sit and watch telly.' She clicked the remote.

Tinkly music immediately filled the room, along with a strident, nasal voice: 'Hoo hoo! Evening, sleepyheads!' Maya and her mum groaned in unison.

'Worst advert EVER!'

warned Maya. 'Quick – change channels!' But in a frantic race to comply, her mum fumbled the remote, batting it upward and away, and it scuttled under the empty chair like a rat with stage fright.

The tinkly music continued, intending to sound soothing but actually sounding like the part in a horror film just before a clown jumps out at you. Then a man appeared on-screen, dressed in an old-fashioned nightgown and cap and holding a candle. 'Bedtime!' he exclaimed into the camera. 'And when you think bedtime – think of Matt! That's me – the owner of Matt's Mattresses!' He winked, prompting another joint groan from Maya and her mum. This advert seemed to be showing every time they turned on the TV and their hatred of it had become a running joke – a way of cheering themselves up during the bleak weeks as they readjusted to a house with only the two of them in it.

'That's a sign from the gods of bad telly,' Maya told her mum decisively, beginning to turn away. 'It is definitely bedtime.'

'Hang on, I'll change it!' Slopping hot chocolate over her fingers, her mum shuffled over to the empty chair and began to search for the remote. 'Give me literally eight seconds.'

Watching her, Maya felt a sudden pang of pity. She wasn't the only person affected by the invisible sadness field, she thought to herself. This was tough on both of them. She hurried over and kneeled to give her mum a quick hug. 'Thanks,' she said, forcing a smile. 'But I'm really heading to bed. I'm wiped out.'

'It's not normal, you know.' Her mum smiled at her. 'A twelve-year-old who wants to go to bed early.'

'Yeah, well, remember what Dad always says?' Maya replied, glancing once again at the empty armchair. 'Who wants to be normal?'

'Fair point,' her mum agreed, breaking off the hug. 'Sleep well. Sweet dreams.'

Maya, who'd been edging away, paused briefly at this. It flitted across her mind that maybe she should talk to her mum some more about the dream she'd had the previous night. But the man in the nightcap on TV was now burbling, 'Matt's Mattresses are the only mattresses with the revolutionary Flamewood Floaty Foam! Formulated by phenomenal physicists, Flamewood Floaty Foam is fashioned from the finest fibres. When you flop on to Flamewood Floaty Foam, you'll feel fantastic!' The irritating voice receded as Maya stumped up the stairs. Reaching the top, she ducked into the bathroom, cutting the man off in mid spiel –

'Floaty Foam!

It's famous!

It's fashionable!

It's f–'

by slamming the door firmly behind her.

The bathroom window looked out on to the Claytons' garden, lit up with the brownish glow of a cloudy, late spring evening. As Maya gazed out of the window while brushing her teeth, a lone ray of sunlight escaped like a pointing finger to land on the large wooden workshop at the end of the garden. Maya released a mint-scented sigh. This long, low building with its cluttered workbenches was where she and her father had spent countless happy hours together. Professor Dexter would usually be busy with piles of paper or a laptop, sitting at his large desk beneath a lit-up neon sign. The sign consisted of six letters – his favourite letters in the entire language, the professor was fond of saying. They spelled out the simple words:

What if?

'The most important question you can ever ask,' he would tell Maya.

He'd set one wall of the workshop aside as Maya's special area. From right back when she was tiny, she had loved to draw. That was what had earned her the nickname used by her father and nobody else – Scribbles. When her teachers complained about exercise books filled with pages and pages of doodles, her father had stood up for her. 'It's just the way her brain works,' he'd explained during one parents' evening, 'and we should never stop a brain from working.' That very night, when they got home, he painted one wall of his workshop white, just for Scribbles, and designated it her Doodle Wall. She had spent hours covering it with fantastical landscapes and creatures: castles, unicorns, spaceships . . . Years of imagination filled the whitewashed planks, all in Maya's thin, spidery style. Now, peering out of the bathroom window, she could dimly make out some of her doodles caught in the evening sunlight. She stared until her eyes prickled, wishing with all her heart that her father was sitting there as he always had done, beneath the sign reading WHAT IF?

Maya heard a loud purring from behind her and turned to see a large and extremely scruffy black cat sitting on the bathroom stool, regarding her calmly with wide green eyes.

'I bet you miss him too, don't you, Bin Bag?' Maya asked the cat, scratching him behind one ear. She had come up with his name when she was small, for the very simple reason that if you scrumpled up a large black bin bag and placed bag and cat side by side, you'd be hard-pressed to tell the difference. No matter how much you groomed him, he always looked untidy and windswept, rather like the hair of a child wizard.

Bin Bag purred even more loudly and followed her into the bedroom, where she changed into her pyjamas and dived beneath her duvet with the grace of a greased penguin slipping beneath an ice floe. Her head was bepillowed and her eyes shut before her black T-shirt – which had been thrown into the air during pyjamarization – had drifted to rest on a nearby chair.

As her mum had quite correctly pointed out, it's not often you find a twelve-year-old as keen to go to bed as Maya Clayton. But that particular night she had a very specific reason for wanting to get to sleep as soon as possible. It was all to do with the dream she'd had the previous night. A very vivid and extremely strange dream that had ended on a very intriguing and extremely annoying cliffhanger. And it had been all about her dad.

We're about to take you nearly twenty-four hours back in time to examine this dream in more detail. But before we do that, there's just one thing we need to clear up.

BORING DREAMS: Our promise to you

We are well aware that other people's dreams are 99.9 per cent boring 99.2 per cent of the time. When someone says to you, 'I had a really weird dream last night,' the chances are it's going to start something like: 'I couldn't find my socks, and I had to put socks on, but I couldn't find them.' Or, 'There was this plant, right? And I had this really strong feeling that it was angry with me for some reason.' At this point the only intelligent response is to stuff your fists over your ears and run away shouting, **'Lalalalalalala, other people's dreams are BORING, shut up, please.'**

We are also aware that we have, in a very real sense, written an entire book that is largely about other people's dreams.

And so, without further adoing, we would like to introduce the Boring Dream Guarantee.

We hereby promise that none of the dreams in this book are boring ones, and none of them are about socks. Well, one of them is, but it's a good one and the socks can talk.

If you find any of the dreams described in this book boring, please make a note of the page number, tie the note on to a cloud and blow it to the following address:

Boring Dream Complaint Department
The Sky

Thank you, and on with the story.

Love,

Gregulent and *Christopherite*

So, with that promise in mind, it's time to leap backwards a few hours and have a peek into Maya's dream from the previous night. So – grab your teddy, snuff out the candle (if you're reading this in Victorian times) and let's begin . . .

DREAM LOG

Creator: Maya Clayton

12 May, 5.41 a.m.

Maya dreamed that she was walking down a long, brightly lit corridor in what she immediately recognized as the hospital where her father was being treated. But it wasn't a part of the building she'd visited before. Plastic signs were suspended from the ceiling pointing off in different directions: X-RAY, DIAGNOSTICS, CANTEEN, BANANA LLAMA DEPARTMENT . . . Yes, you read that correctly. This is a dream, don't forget. Some very odd things can crop up in dreams. Most hospitals don't have a Banana Llama Department, but this one, apparently, did. Intrigued, Maya followed the arrow on the sign and pushed open a swing door that led into a large room with a spick-and-span reception desk just inside.

'Hello,' said the smartly dressed llama sitting behind the desk, without looking up. 'Just pop them over there with the others, would you?'

Maya craned her neck to look beyond the llama, and saw that the rest of the room was almost filled by several large wooden crates with the words LLAMA BANANAS branded diagonally on to them. She coughed meekly. 'Um, I'm sorry, but I don't have any bananas for you,' she said.

'Well, why are you in here, then?' replied the llama sharply, peering up at her over thin spectacles that were fastened round its long neck by a thin silver chain.

'I just wanted to have a look around,' replied Maya.

'Wait a moment,' said the llama, reaching up with a hoof and snatching off its spectacles. 'You're not even a llama!'

'**0-oh . . .**' stuttered Maya. 'Sorry, I . . . I didn't realize it was llamas only.'

'Of course it's llamas only,' said the llama officiously. Maya was starting to realize that it was one of those rather stern llamas with a little too much respect for rules and regulations. A real jobsworth, not to put too fine a point on it. 'Llamas and bananas – it's very simple,' it continued, 'and if you don't leave immediately, I shall sound the alarm. The banana llama alarm.'

'I'm very sorry,' said Maya in her most llama-mollifying tone of voice. 'I didn't mean to alarm a llama, or alarm a banana llama. I mean –'

But it was too late. The llama reached out its hoof and firmly pressed an enormous yellow button that protruded from the very centre of the desk. At once, a hideously loud bleating filled the room, and violently yellow lights strobed on the walls and ceilings. Maya turned for the door and ran.

As she sprinted back towards the main passageway the piercing bleating noise began to fade slightly. But before she could relax, Maya realized that it had been replaced by another, even more ominous sound. A heavy clopping noise, which seemed to be getting louder.

Being chased is one of the most frightening things that can happen in a dream. It gives you a weird buzzing sensation in your legs, right? Well, imagine Maya's horror when she glanced over her shoulder to see an entire troupe of llamas galloping after her. Is troupe the right word? Well, anyway, it was a lot of llamas, neighing and mooing frantically

as they stampeded towards her. And, yes, possibly those aren't the exact noises that llamas make, but this is a dream, remember? Also it's our book, so we can do what we like.

Maya fled down corridor after corridor, with the uneasy feeling that the long, bare passageways were extending ahead of her like an unfolding telescope. She pelted round corners, skidding on the polished hospital floors, and gradually the

bleating, **NEIGHING** and **clopping**
subsided as the banana llama army was left
behind. Maya looked around and suddenly
realized she knew exactly where she was. She
was in the same hospital corridor she had
been in – awake – earlier that very same day.
It was the hospital corridor where her dad was
being kept. 'I wonder if he'll still be here?' she
wondered, aware on some level that this was
a dream.

But if I'm asleep . . . thought Maya to herself, *I wonder if he might be awake?* Excitedly, she rushed to the last door on the left and threw it open.

Up until now, Maya's dream had been fairly uninteresting. Yes, we know it had llamas in it and everything, but that's fairly standard weird-dream stuff. It was when she stepped into her father's hospital room that things got really strange.

When you encounter a familiar room within a dream, it's often different in a subtle way that you don't immediately notice. Over the past six weeks Maya had spent hours and hours in this room and she was familiar with every tiny part of it: the frosted-glass windows, the two uncomfortable plasticky yellow chairs in the corner by the wall-mounted TV, the stand that held the bags and tubes connected to the metal hospital bed, the **peeping** and **bleeping** machines that monitored her dad as he slept on and on, baffling the doctors.

Because that was what was wrong with Professor Dexter: he was fast asleep. According to all the doctors' tests, he was completely healthy. He was just fast asleep, and couldn't be woken up.

In Maya's dream, the professor's hospital room looked almost identical to the one she saw every day when she visited him – with two rather important differences. Firstly, the professor wasn't in it. The bed was empty – the sheets and blankets neatly folded down and tucked in, hospital corners and everything. And the second difference was the complete stranger who was sitting on one of the chairs in the corner. It was a teenage boy that Maya had never seen before in her life.

He had scruffy orange hair and even scruffier and orangier shoes, propped up casually on the other plastic chair. Hair and shoes were all Maya could see to start with, because the boy was facing away from her watching the TV, which appeared to be showing a football match between two teams of penguins. This is all happening inside a dream, remember? 'Er, hello?' said Maya uncertainly.

The boy spoke without turning round. 'About time, too. I've been waiting here for hours. And these penguins are really rubbish at football.' As he spoke, one of the penguins tripped over the ball and skidded along the pitch on its tummy.

Maya was well aware that simply saying, 'What?' in reply to this would be very much the default response. But her dream-foggy brain was unable to think of anything more cutting. 'What?' she said faintly, looking again at the empty bed.

At this, the boy turned round. He had an

expression on his face that his parents would probably have described as either impish or cheeky, while his teachers would have preferred the word infuriating or – in the privacy of the staff room – something rather ruder. It was the smug expression of a cat that had got the cream, but only if the cream in question was yours and the cat was drinking it in front of you while singing a mocking song about how delicious it was.

'You must be Maya,' said the boy, grinning. 'Hello.'

'Did you say you'd been *waiting* for me?'

'Yeah,' the boy confirmed, taking his legs off the second chair and kicking it around so she could sink down opposite him.

'Waiting . . .
INSIDE my dream?'

'Yeah,' he repeated, clearly relishing the feeling of being the one holding all the cards. 'What's with all the llamas?'

'You . . . you saw them?' Maya asked, nervously straining her ears for any faint clop or moo.

'They galloped past the door earlier on, yeah,' said the boy airily. 'Mind you, dreams are strange places, right? Before I found yours, I wandered into your next-door neighbour's by accident. He was dreaming about the North Pole, and it was freezing in there.' He raised his tangerine eyebrows.

'Sorry.' Maya held up a hand. 'Did you say you wandered into a *dream*?'

'Well, yeah,' said the boy. 'Thanks to your dad, of course.'

Maya stared at him, dumbstruck. How could this strange boy, who had unexpectedly turned up in the middle of her own dream, possibly know about her dad's research? Because Professor Dexter was, indeed, one of the world's foremost experts on dreams. For weeks before his accident he'd been promising Maya that he had made a breakthrough and couldn't wait to share it with her. But then there'd been that dreadful phone call. Maya frowned in her sleep as, even mid dream, the painful memory returned: her mum's face shocked and confused as she spoke into the handset. 'An accident? How? What happened? He's unconscious?'

Maya felt like she'd been hit in the stomach with a giant sock stuffed with electric eels. 'You know about my dad's research?' she asked quietly.

'Yeah.'

Maya was beginning to feel that if this boy said 'yeah' one more time, she would actually reach over and do something rather painful to all the different parts of his face at the same time. She missed her dad so badly it felt like a part of her brain was missing – and, if this strange boy knew something, she wanted answers, not smart replies.

'We've been **BEEP** to rescue him **BEEP BEEP**.

Oh no, is that the time already?' the boy continued.

'To what?' asked Maya desperately. 'Rescue him? What's happening?' The boy, and the room around him, seemed to be slowly dissolving.

'Your alarm – **BEEP** – your alarm's going off **BEEPITY BEEP**. You're waking up. I'll come back tonight **BEEP** and explain everything.'

As Maya watched, the boy's face and the hospital room melted away into darkness, leaving only the beeping noise. Groaning, she reached out and hit the snooze button on her bedside clock with what was probably unnecessary force.

She opened her eyes to see Bin Bag curled up on the chair by her bed. He raised his head and peered at her. 'Well, that was exceptionally annoying,' she told the cat, who blinked slowly in reply.

'Morning,' said her mum brightly, poking her head round the door. 'Sleep well? Any good dreams?' It was the question that Maya's dad used to ask her eagerly every morning, and the image of the empty hospital bed came sharply back to her, along with the very unexpected word that boy had used: rescue.

'I dreamed about dad's hospital room,' she said sleepily.

'That's probably because we're going to visit him later,' her mum replied.

'He isn't there, though,' mumbled Maya, flecks of the dream still clustering round her head like brightly coloured mist.

'What?' said her mum, opening the door wider. 'What do you mean, he's not there?'

Maya sat up and shook her head. 'Sorry, I was having a really bizarre dream. I think. Unless the house is full of llamas.'

'Oh, sure. They're all downstairs waiting for their breakfast. Why don't you come and join them? Llamas love a scrambled egg.'

'Actually, I think they prefer bananas,' said Maya to herself as she swung her legs out of bed and began to hunt for her school uniform.

CHAPTER 2
THE SLEEPING PROFESSOR

Maya Clayton was a daydreamer. Oh, sure, she was a night-dreamer as well, as we've just discovered. But she was also a big fan of slipping into her own world when she was awake. To help her do this, she would often pull the hood of her favourite coat right up round her head. It was a large, fluffy hood and when it was fully deployed it reduced the real world to a manageable circle. Inside, Maya could click off reality like a boring TV show and flick through her own imagination instead. It was much more entertaining and, since her dad's accident, far more cheerful too.

As she walked to school, Maya was battling the constant sensation that she hadn't properly woken up.

Hood firmly raised against an unusually cold morning, she plodded along on autopilot, mind firmly elsewhere. The dream about the stranger in her dad's hospital room had been so real, so vivid.

Who WAS he?

She was convinced she'd never seen him in real life – his bright orange hair and that impish, mocking expression wouldn't easily be forgotten. Was it even possible, Maya thought to herself as she trudged through the school gates, to dream about someone you'd never seen before? Surely dreams came out of your own brain. How on earth had this slightly annoying stranger got in there?

'Hey, Maya!'

'Morning!'

She swivelled her hood-periscope to see a group of her friends hanging around by the gates, but she simply waved vaguely and walked on. 'Guess we'll see you later, then?' she heard one of them call after her, but she didn't reply. Since her dad's accident, Maya had been less and less talkative, and was spending less and less time with her friends. It was just so hard, dealing with all those concerned questions. Especially when there was no good news to impart. Having to tell them, 'He's still asleep. The doctors still don't know what's wrong. No, I don't know if he'll wake up,' made it all far too real. It was easier to say nothing.

Maya skulked into the first lesson of the day – double geography – and slumped down at a desk in the back row, hood still raised like a barrier against the real world. It didn't help that this was her least favourite subject, although, to be fair, it could have been a double art lesson – her favourite – followed by after-school pizza-and-chips-eating club and she'd still have been feeling rubbish. But she needed some time to think.

Once again, she reran in her head the day she'd found out about her dad's accident. Once again, she saw her mum on the phone. 'How did this happen? Where have they taken him? Do you think he'll –' At this point she had caught sight of Maya hovering anxiously in the kitchen doorway and rapidly switched whatever the end of that sentence was going to be to, 'That is . . . do you think we'll be able to visit him straight away?'

Maya had waited until the end of the call, knowing full well that the awful details that were pouring into her mum's ear were about to be filtered and passed down to her with as much added positivity as possible.

'There's been an accident,' her mum told her a few moments later, 'but I really don't want you to worry . . .'

Remembering that moment now, Maya snorted through her nose in frustration, making the pages of the geography textbook in front of her flutter. That Tuesday six weeks ago had undoubtedly been the worst day of her life – being told the professor's equipment

had malfunctioned . . .

that he wouldn't wake up . . .

that he'd be kept in hospital while they ran tests.

Maya hardly noticed when the teacher bustled in and announced they'd be continuing their study of coastal erosion. He scanned the class, sighing slightly when he caught sight of Maya still buried inside her hood in the back row. She'd always been prone to disappearing off into her own world at times, but since her father's accident it seemed she'd decided to relocate there permanently.

Maya tuned out as the lesson began. Even the teacher's excited announcement,

'I've made up a RAP about wave-cut platforms!'

didn't bring her back to reality. She felt like she was trying to put a jigsaw together in her head, but it was a thousand-piece puzzle and she had, at most, half of the pieces. And no corners or edges.

A professor studying dreams. An accident at the laboratory. He wouldn't wake up. And now, talk of a rescue . . .

Suddenly Maya jerked upright, the hood falling

away from her head. 'Ah, I thought my rap might get your attention!' said the teacher, delighted to have broken through. But Maya wasn't looking at him. The classroom door was open and she had been gazing vacantly at the gaggle of latecomers trailing down the corridor. And among them, she had caught a flash of bright orange shoes scuffing past.

Ignoring the teacher's shout, Maya jumped to her feet and raced out of the classroom, elbowing her way into the throng and looking left and right for the ginger-haired boy from her dream, as students drained away round corners and into classrooms like bathwater down multiple plugholes.

At the end of the corridor Maya caught sight of the orange shoes again, disappearing round a bend, and pelted off in pursuit.

Skidding on the tiled floor, she grabbed the shoe-wearer by the shoulder and spun them round.

But the shocked face now confronting her was not that of the red-headed boy.

It was a girl she recognized, one of the COOLEST in the whole school.

She was several years above Maya, liked by everyone and even captain of the football team.

'OY!'

she spat at Maya, in angry surprise. 'What do you think you're playing at?'

'Sorry,' Maya mumbled sheepishly. 'I thought you were someone else.' Pausing to ineffectually smooth down the lapels of the girl's school blazer, she squeaked into a 180-degree turn and headed back towards her classroom.

'Weirdo!' the girl shot after her.

'Thanks,' replied Maya automatically. It was another habit she'd picked up from her dad. As someone who usually shambled about the place with a long stripy scarf wound round his neck, quite often muttering to himself, the professor got the odd remark like that too. And he always greeted them with warm gratitude.

'If anyone ever calls you a weirdo, or an oddball, anything like that,' he explained to Maya once, 'they're paying you a huge compliment. They're telling you that you're different to the rest of the herd, and that's a truly wonderful thing to be.'

'If you've quite finished your little walkabout,' the geography teacher said sardonically when Maya shouldered her way back into the classroom, mumbling a brief apology and slumping at her desk, 'we'll continue, shall we?'

Maya reached a hand back over her head and pulled up the hood of her coat, attempting to shut the real world out once again as the teacher began to beatbox:

'I'm a wave-cut platform – **YO**, what's the **COMMOTION**?

It's the sea on my rocks, and that's **COASTAL EROSION**.'

*

After school, Maya trailed out of the main doors, hood up and ignoring further friendly shouts on either side. 'Chin up!' came a voice as she ambled across the front yard like a zombie. Maya's mum was leaning out of the car window, looking at her quizzically. Maya lifted her gaze and forced a smile.

'Come on,' her mum told her, 'let's go and see how he's doing. Maybe today's the day we get some good news.'

As they drove to the hospital Maya gazed gloomily out of the window, allowing the lamp posts flashing past to lull her into a kind of doze. Her head slumped against the cool glass of the window, and when the car pulled through the tall iron gates, she gazed through half-closed eyes at the large sign fixed to them. HAGSTONE COURT, it read. HEALTH, SECLUSION, SECURITY. Not for the first time, Maya mused that 'security' was a strange word for a private hospital to include in its mission statement. But her mum had told her that Hagstone Court was very exclusive and very, very expensive. And her dad's boss had insisted on paying for all his medical care.

'Let's go and talk to Doctor Lara,' her mum said, parking on the gravel area in front of the modern glass front doors. 'See if she's got those test results back.'

'Doctor Llama?' asked Maya, still feeling befuddled.

She climbed out of the car and trailed after her mum. They gave their names at reception, and were escorted by a nurse to the wing where her father was being treated. They passed a sign reading X-RAY and Maya looked around wildly for the one saying BANANA LLAMA DEPARTMENT. *Don't be silly*, she told herself. *That was a dream. Right?*

The nurse punched numbers into a set of large metal doors, which clanged open, and soon they were walking down the same familiar corridor Maya had seen almost every day for the past six weeks. She couldn't help wondering whether the room would be empty – the dream had seemed so real – and even whether the boy with the orange shoes would be there, feet up, watching penguin football.

But the room wasn't empty. Her dad was there, same as always, with the same **beeping** and **peeping** machines and the same cascade of wires and tubes. Maya got the same pang she did every time she came here. The figure in the bed just didn't look like her dad, without his large wire-rimmed spectacles and the long stripy scarf he always wore – his Thinking Scarf, as he called it. It was folded neatly on the bedside table, with the glasses on top, looking forlorn and lonely despite its cheery purple and green stripes. Bare-faced and bare-necked, the figure asleep in the bed looked far more vulnerable than her confident, capable father.

The boy from her dream wasn't in the room, of course, as this wasn't a dream. But someone else was – a tall, angular woman in a smart black suit. She was standing over Maya's dad, holding a small, rather wilted-looking bunch of flowers in one hand and staring at him intently. Her dark, straight-cut hair had fallen forward over her face; she was bending her head, apparently listening to his breathing.

Maya's mum gave a small cough and the woman flinched, but then she caught herself. She straightened up slowly. 'Tess!' she exclaimed, smiling. 'And this must be your daughter! Hello. Come in, come in.'

'Hello, Lilith.' Maya's mum bristled slightly at being invited into her own husband's hospital room. 'What brings you here?'

'Oh, well, you know . . .' The woman brandished the flowers, which she was gripping rather tightly. A small bloom gave up the struggle and fell on to the blanket with a tiny **plip**. 'I wanted to see how our star scientist was doing.'

Maya recognized the name, of course. Lilith Delamere was the head of the company where her dad worked, Somnia Incorporated. But for someone who ran a sleep-science laboratory, Lilith Delamere didn't look like she was great at the practical side of things, i.e. actually sleeping. Her eyes were ringed with dark circles like an insomniac panda, as if, thought Maya to herself, she hadn't slept in weeks. No, more than that.

In YEARS.

'So – no change?' asked Lilith, bending over the patient once again. Maya couldn't stop herself taking a protective step forward.

'Let's not crowd him,' she heard herself say. Something about the way Lilith Delamere was possessively hovering over her dad unnerved her.

Lilith held up a hand and took a step back, regarding Maya coolly. 'Well, I'll find somewhere to put these,' she said, waving the limp flowers around again.

Try the bin, answered Maya coldly – but only in her head. There are limits to how rude you can be to your parents' bosses, even in a hospital setting.

'Ah, everyone's here,' said a voice from the doorway. Maya turned to see her dad's consultant, smart in her white coat, a stethoscope swinging round her neck. Maya's brain filled with thoughts of llamas again and she had to do a massive double take when she saw a banana sticking out of the doctor's top pocket. 'Little snack for later,' the consultant said, seeing Maya staring. 'Hello,' she continued, looking across at Lilith. 'I don't think we've met. I'm Doctor Lara Cross.'

'Lilith Delamere,' said the taller woman, marching over and holding out her hand as if she owned the place. 'Do come in, doctor. What's the update?'

'Well,' said Doctor Lara, glancing uncertainly at Maya's mum, who nodded at her, as if to signal, *Yes, you can discuss my husband with this bossy woman who's just invited you into a room in your own hospital,* 'there's no improvement, I'm sorry to say.'

'No sign of his waking up at all?' said Lilith, patting the blankets. 'Oh dear, dear.' She reached out and took a grape from the bowl on the bedside table, popping it into her mouth and munching. Still chewing, she turned to Maya with a pitying expression. 'You must miss him terribly,' she said, cocking her head to one side.

Maya stared back at her, nonplussed. How was she supposed to answer that? Wasn't it obvious? Gradually she became aware that the whole room had fallen silent while Lilith waited for an answer – there was only the **humming** and **beeping** of the machines.

'Of course I do,' Maya snapped suddenly, more sharply than she'd intended.

'Maya!' her mum scolded her. 'Be nice! Lilith's come all this way to check up on your father!' *And she's paying for this posh hospital*, her raised eyebrows added silently.

'It's fine,' soothed Lilith, patting Maya patronizingly on the cheek. 'She's understandably stressed, poor little lamb. It's a lot for young brains to cope with.' Maya fumed and glared at Lilith, who gave a thin smile and smoothed down her smart skirt. 'Well, I'll leave you to it, doctor . . . carry on.' Doctor Lara again looked a little startled to be given instructions in her own hospital by a total stranger.

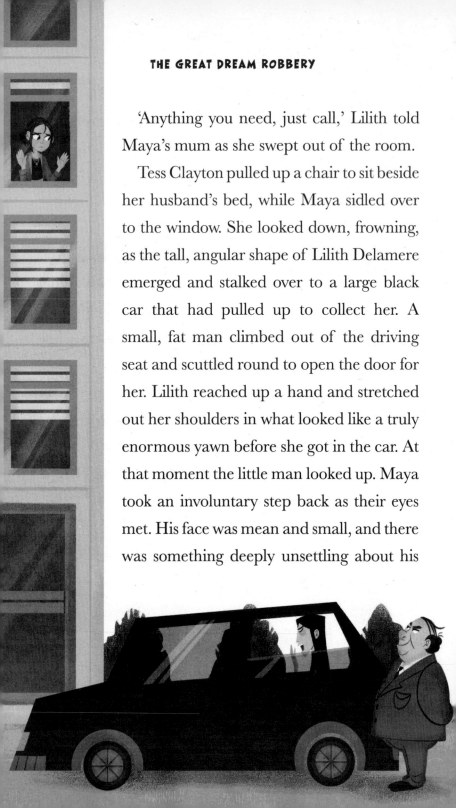

'Anything you need, just call,' Lilith told Maya's mum as she swept out of the room.

Tess Clayton pulled up a chair to sit beside her husband's bed, while Maya sidled over to the window. She looked down, frowning, as the tall, angular shape of Lilith Delamere emerged and stalked over to a large black car that had pulled up to collect her. A small, fat man climbed out of the driving seat and scuttled round to open the door for her. Lilith reached up a hand and stretched out her shoulders in what looked like a truly enormous yawn before she got in the car. At that moment the little man looked up. Maya took an involuntary step back as their eyes met. His face was mean and small, and there was something deeply unsettling about his small, complacent smile – it was the face of a man who knows something unpleasant is going on . . . and likes it. Abruptly, he turned on his heel and crunched back to the front of the car.

Maya stored it all away in her growing mental jigsaw puzzle. The sleeping professor. The boss who looked like she never rested checking up on him. The hospital that boasted about security. And, most of all, the boy in her dream the previous night who had talked about a rescue.

Maya was growing more certain by the second that whatever had happened to her father had not been an accident, and she itched to go back to sleep in case the boy who seemed to have at least some of the answers appeared in her dreams once more.

*

'Ten minutes! Come on, please, just another ten minutes!'

'**No!**'

'Oh . . . *please*? . . . All right, then – five minutes. Just five more minutes!'

Yes, we're back where we came in. Maya's desperate to go to bed, and even if you are too, don't stop reading now, OK? We're coming up to a really good bit, even if we do say so ourselves.

Sorry, that probably came across as a bit cocky, didn't it? I mean, we think it's a good bit. You might hate it. Let's all carry on reading for a bit, then we'll compare notes, shall we?

Onward.

After she'd jumped into bed, and said goodnight to Bin Bag in her usual way, Maya was asleep within seconds. And this time, she found herself back in the dream almost immediately. It was almost as if she'd left a film on pause and was picking up exactly where she'd left off. And that was lucky, because she managed to bypass the whole llama section, which had, frankly, been weird. She heard a faint **bleat** in the background but that was it.

DREAM LOG

Creator: Maya Clayton
12 May, 10.18 p.m.

To her relief, Maya found herself standing outside the door of her dad's hospital room once again. She took a brief second to congratulate herself. *Excellent dreaming, Maya,* she said silently. *Now we'll find out what's going on.* She pushed the door open, finding the bed empty, as she'd expected, but, to be honest, she only gave the bed the briefest of glances. She was looking at the chairs in the corner, and sure enough the same battered orange trainers were propped up and the same penguin football match was playing on the TV. Or at least a similar one. It was hard to tell.

'**OY!**' shouted Maya, plunging through the door.

'**ORANGE-SHOE BOY!**

Where's **MY DAD?**

What's going on?

What's your message?

How did **YOU** get here?

How are you in my dream?

Why are those penguins playing football?

What's going on?

QUICK, **QUICK**, before I wake up again!'

The boy swung himself out of the chair and stood up to face her. 'Welcome back,' he said drily. 'Take a seat, why don't you?'

'There isn't time!' Maya said desperately and very, very fast. 'Last night you were just about to tell me something really bizarre and then you started beeping, and then I woke up. And I'm really stressed about my dad, so sorry for speaking at, like, a hundred miles an hour, but do you know something about him? *Please!*'

'Sheesh, you really are stressed out, aren't you?' said the boy. 'For someone who's asleep, you're very cranky. You need to get some rest.'

'But I am resting!' wailed a frustrated Maya. 'I'm asleep!'

'In that case,' said the boy, 'why don't you sit down and let me explain? This will all make sense, I promise.'

Reluctantly, Maya sank into the chair opposite the boy, who also sat down, now placing his scuffed orange shoes on a low table that stood between them. He grabbed the remote and muted the TV, so the commentary on the penguin football match disappeared. Maya was briefly disappointed because one of the penguins was about to take a penalty, but she managed to focus.

'So why are the penguins playing football?' she blurted out. It wasn't the most important question on her list, but it was uppermost in her mind. Well, it would be, wouldn't it?

'You tell me,' said the boy and grinned rather infuriatingly. 'It's your dream.'

'OK, so if it's my dream, what are you doing in it?' asked Maya, now getting on to the more useful questions.

'Now, *that* question,' said the boy, 'has a much more interesting answer.' He re-crossed his legs, apparently enjoying the suspense, before catching sight of Maya's furious face.

'OK, OK,' he promised, 'I'm explaining.'

'Explain,' pleaded Maya, 'more quickly. This is something to do with my dad's research, right? He told me he was close to some kind of breakthrough. Something to do with dreams.'

The boy took a deep breath. 'Listen,' he told her, 'I've entered your dream using a NAP chair based on your dad's invention, which is codenamed CHEESE.'

'Cheese?' Maya blurted.

'That's CRACKERS!'

'You're over-excited, so I'll let that one slide,' said the boy magnanimously. 'Professor Dexter has been trapped inside his own dream and we need your help to find him.'

There was SILENCE.

On-screen, a penguin was red-carded after a dangerous sliding tackle.

'Now explain that explanation,' said Maya, 'more slowly.'

'Your dad,' he said, doing that annoying boy thing of speaking in an exaggeratedly loud and slow voice, 'did an invention, yeah? He invented a thing. Understand?'

'You,' Maya told him, 'are extremely annoying. Did you know?'

'Yes,' said the boy, 'I am well aware of this. Thank you.'

'Well . . . how do you know my dad?'

'Our mum works with him,' explained the boy. 'I'm Teddy, by the way. Teddy Flamewood.'

'Flamewood?' Maya echoed. 'What, like the mattress man? In the terrible adverts?'

Teddy looked slightly embarrassed at this. 'Yeah,' he admitted reluctantly. 'They're fairly cringe-worthy, sorry. That's our dad.'

'Not at all.' Maya grinned at him. 'It's like meeting a celebrity. "Flamewood Floaty Foam,"' she mimicked.

'All right, all right.' Teddy held up his hands in surrender. 'And you'll meet my sister soon, too. She's called Bea.' He paused for a moment, as if listening, and added, 'She says hello. And that she's looking forward to it. And that I should stop flannelling about and explain this to you properly.'

'I wholeheartedly agree,' said Maya, who felt that Teddy had enjoyed his moment of holding all the cards for quite long enough. This was her dream, after all.

Suddenly, Teddy looked serious. 'You're being watched,' he told Maya, who jumped and turned round in her chair, wondering wildly if she'd see a llama eyeing her from the doorway. 'No, not here,' Teddy explained. 'I mean in actual life – when you're awake.'

'Watched? Why? By who? And if you correct that to "whom" I shall come over there and kick your face off.'

'Fair enough.' Teddy shrugged. 'Listen – do you know a woman called Lilith Delamere?'

Even though Maya had been half expecting this question, it still threw her. Once again she saw Lilith Delamere bending over her sleeping father in mock-concern. And the face of the small, fat man flew back into her mind as well, with his smug, scheming expression.

'She was here today,' she told Teddy Flamewood. 'Well, not *here* here . . . but in this room. In the awake version of it.'

'Checking up on him, most likely,' he replied grimly. 'Making sure he's out of action.'

'You mean – she did this to him?' Maya's stomach flared with rage. 'She's keeping him asleep?'

'**BINGO**, bravo, **eureka**, **CORRECT**-a-mundo and ten points to Gryffindor,'

replied Teddy. 'Your dad's invention allows you to enter people's dreams.'

Maya gaped. She knew her dad had been researching dreams, but she had never imagined he'd actually invented a way to get inside them. 'Enter . . . dreams?' she repeated weakly.

'Yup,' Teddy confirmed. 'It's what Bea and I are using right now to contact you. But somehow Lilith trapped the professor inside a dream. That's why he can't wake up.'

'But if you can be in my dream,' Maya wanted to know, 'why can't you just go into his dream instead and wake him up?'

'Ah.' Teddy held up a finger. 'Well, that was our plan. But we've hit a problem, and we need your help. Only thing is, you'll have to keep it completely secret. Don't even tell your mum, OK? Like I said, you're being watched. Both of you. And these people are ruthless.'

'Got it,' said Maya, feeling frightened and excited at the same time. Frightcited, if you like. If this meant she could help her dad, she would do whatever it took. 'What do you need me to do?'

'You need to sneak out and meet Bea and me in the real world,' explained Teddy. 'Tomorrow night, wait till your mum's asleep . . .'

The following morning Maya sat bolt upright in bed, with the morning sun streaming through the blinds and the alarm clock bleeping its face off beside her. Eyes wide, she turned to Bin Bag, who was sitting on his usual chair.

'You are not going to believe what happened in my dream,' Maya told him, trying to identify the unfamiliar feeling in her chest. After a moment she realized: it was hope. 'I've got to write these instructions down before I forget.' Bin Bag watched as she scrabbled in the bedside drawer for a pencil and paper.

(So what did you think? It was a good bit, wasn't it?)

CHAPTER 3
SOMNIA INCORPORATED

'Welcome to the Heptagon . . . headquarters of Somnia Incorporated,' said Lilith Delamere's own recorded voice to her as the automatic glass doors slid smoothly open.

The Heptagon, as the geometrically minded among you will have worked out already, was a large, white, seven-sided building. It stood alone, in the middle of a series of lawns so carefully manicured that they looked artificial. Rigidly pruned shrubs stood here and there, clipped into severe cubes.

Lilith paused for a moment just inside the doors to survey her domain. The large reception area was mainly bare, furnished only with a few rows of the sort of hard plastic chairs that look as if they have a grudge against bottoms. A single receptionist sat behind the long, white desk at the other side of the room, dressed in a smart white lab coat, as if he were a scientist. Lilith insisted all her staff wore them – she wanted the few visitors she admitted to her HQ to be in no doubt that this was a place of research.

Once again, Lilith had hardly slept the night before. The bags beneath her eyes were so big they were more like suitcases. You see, every time Lilith Delamere went to sleep, she was woken up again by a horrible nightmare. A nightmare about one particular thing. A thing that was waiting for her inside this pristine white building.

As you can imagine, the constant lack of a proper night's sleep meant that Lilith was not the nicest of bosses. In fact, she was probably the least nicest. She was in a constant bad mood that sloshed around inside her like filthy water in a bucket, threatening at any moment to slop out on to anyone unlucky enough to find themself nearby. Pausing to give her forty-fifth huge yawn of the day so far – it was 8.49 a.m., by the way – she began to walk across towards reception, her polished heels smacking the floor as if it had offended them in some way. But halfway across the room she stopped. The receptionist, who had been watching her nervously, gulped and adjusted the collar of his white coat to let out a warm gust of anxiety.

'What,' said Lilith, her voice rebounding from the bare white walls so it could slap the receptionist in the ears from several different directions at once, 'is this?' She stooped to pick up a small piece of crumpled paper, which she held aloft accusingly.

'I . . . I . . . ahm . . .' The man behind reception was panicking. 'I'm not altogether sure.'

Lilith stalked towards him like an enraged heron, holding the scrap of paper away from her as if it might explode at any moment. 'This,' she hissed, pressing it towards his face.

'What is THIS?'

'I believe it's a **pah**,

a **pah**,

a **pah**

pah . . .'

Lilith's ferocity had completely severed the connection between the man's brain and his mouth.

'It's a **pah**,

a piece of **pah**,

of **pah** . . .

pah . . .'

he gibbered, so petrified that sweat had actually started to come out of one of his eyelashes. 'It's a piece of **pah** . . . of paper,' he finally managed to gasp.

There was a moment of silence, punctuated only by a small **plip** as a gobbet of sweat left his eyelash and fell on to the highly polished desk.

Lilith bent forward until she was almost nose to nose with the terrified receptionist. 'This,' she told him, in a voice colder than a penguin's posterior, 'is a scientific laboratory. Not a gigantic wastepaper basket.'

The man nodded like a novelty dog on the back shelf of a car as it's going over a hill. 'Yes, Ms Delamere. Absolutely. It won't happen again.'

'No,' agreed Lilith icily. 'It most certainly will not.'

She jerked upright and marched through the doors to one side of the desk. A light blinked green as she approached and the doors slid smoothly open. Once again her own recorded voice oozed out of the speakers: 'Access granted. Welcome to Somnia. Sleep well.' Lilith winced.

While the receptionist sat back and mopped his eyelashes in relief, Lilith clipped down a long white corridor, the doors hissing closed behind her as she headed towards the lifts. This passageway wasn't quite as sparse as the reception area. Lilith had read somewhere that art in the workplace could be good for productivity, so the walls were occasionally punctuated by white canvases decorated with geometric black shapes. Yes, we know. Not especially inspiring. But Lilith wasn't a fan of colours. In fact there were only two places in the entire Heptagon where colours were permitted. You're about to see one of them in two paragraphs' time. The other will be revealed later in the story, cos it's exciting and cool.

'Seventh floor. Executive level.' The lift doors parted and, in a few seconds, Lilith was slumping gratefully into a comfortable leather chair behind her enormous desk. A comfortable, black leather chair, just to be clear. And the desk was white. But on the wall behind Lilith was the patch of colour which we mentioned in the last paragraph and which is going to be fully described in the next one, which is starting . . .

wait for it . . .

DOCTOR DAMIAN DELAMERE

Hanging on the wall behind Lilith's desk was a huge oil painting of a smartly suited man with thinning hair, narrow eyes and a pinched, lined face. At first glance he looked like a fairly unpleasant man. But then at second glance you realized he was, in fact, a *hugely* unpleasant man. At first glance he looked like the sort of man who, if he lived next door to you and you accidentally kicked a ball into his garden, wouldn't throw it back. But then at second glance you realized that he would, in fact, probably pop the ball with a garden fork and then set it on fire in front of you just to see the look on your face. And laugh. The more you looked at that painting, the more you got the impression that the man it depicted was staring right back at you, and hating you with all the enthusiasm of a professional hater who's about to take part in a globally recognized hating competition. And the prize for the hatiest hater is a billion pounds and a lifetime's supply of . . . something hatey people like. Those pink wafer biscuits, probably.

The frame round the painting was ornate and golden. It couldn't have fitted in less with the decor at Somnia Incorporated if it had been shocking neon pink. And at the bottom of the frame was a small plaque, bearing the words: DOCTOR DAMIAN DELAMERE, FOUNDER OF SOMNIA INCORPORATED.

**Yes, yes.
Calm down,
Sherlock Holmes.**

He's got the same surname as Lilith. We don't just make this stuff up on the spot, you know. The nasty-looking man in the oil painting was, indeed, Lilith's late father. He was late in the sense of being no longer alive. Ironically, he had had impeccable time-keeping, when he was alive. Doctor Damian Delamere had been incredibly proud of himself for never being late for anything, ever. And if you'd been late for a meeting with him, he'd have immediately had you sacked. Imagine having that for a dad. Almost makes you feel sorry for Lilith, doesn't it? Well, OK, not quite. But at least we tried.

Doctor Damian Delamere had left his laboratory to his only child – his daughter. Which sounds like a nice thing to do. But, as with so many things in his life, he'd managed to do it in a nasty way. 'You'll never make a success of this laboratory,' he used to say to young Lilith as he grew older, dodderier and yet still nastier. 'I wish there were someone else to take over. Someone with at least an inkling of the necessary intelligence and drive. But you're all I've got, unfortunately.' Unsurprisingly, Lilith had never bought him one of those mugs saying

WORLD'S GREATEST DAD

on Fathers' Day. If there'd been one saying

WORLD'S MEANEST DAD WHO CONSTANTLY MAKES ME FEEL ABOUT THREE MILLIMETRES TALL – BUT IS AT LEAST ALWAYS PROMPT,

she'd have bought that – but they don't make them; thankfully there isn't the demand. And no one's made a mug big enough to fit all those words on, anyway; it would be more like a bucket.

Remember we told you that Lilith wasn't a fan of colours? Even that's down to her horrible dad. Once, when she was an excited, newly qualified scientist, she had turned up for work at this laboratory in a brand-new, bright red dress she'd bought specially for her first day at work. Doctor Damian had taken one long, frosty look at her and ordered her to go home and change. 'This is a place of scientific research,' he had sneered as she slunk out, face now as red as her expensive dress, 'not a fancy-dress party.'

'Fancy-dress party indeed,' Lilith muttered angrily to herself, before the sleek white speaker on her sleek white desk broke into her reverie. 'Good morning, Ms Delamere,' said a disembodied voice. Lilith, almost able to feel her oil-painting father's disapproving gaze on the back of her neck, winced slightly before replying.

'Yes?' she snapped, pushing a small switch with a manicured finger.

'Your nine a.m. appointment is waiting for you,' replied the voice.

Lilith sighed, not bothering to take her finger off the switch, so her assistant could share her frustration.

'Very well,' she said grudgingly, 'send them up. And then tell General Pheare I need to see him urgently.'

'At once, Ms Delamere.'

After a few moments the lift doors opened and a white-coated woman stepped rather meekly into the office.

'Yes, yes, come in. What is it?' Lilith asked sharply. The woman came forward, looking left and right as if she might be asked to sit down, but the only chair in the room was the large leather one from which Lilith was now glaring at her. 'Well?' she prompted.

The woman coughed. 'Good morning, Ms Delamere,' she began, and waited briefly for a polite answer. It became apparent immediately that it wasn't going to arrive, so she ploughed on. 'My name's Catherine – and I'm one of your technicians from the research division on the fourth floor. I've been speaking with a few of my colleagues, and we've decided to ask you whether . . . that is to say . . .' She was starting to wilt a little in the chilly ferocity of Lilith's stare, but, like an Antarctic explorer of old determined to reach the South Pole, she pressed on. 'We wanted to ask you whether it might be possible to have a break room.'

Lilith's stare became, if possible, even icier. If Catherine from the fourth floor actually had been an Antarctic explorer of old, this would have been the part of the mission where they start saying things like, 'I'm going outside now and I may be some time.'

'A break . . . room,' Lilith repeated, deadpan.

'That's right. You know, nothing fancy. Just a couple of more comfortable chairs. Maybe a kettle, or even a little coffee machine. Just for . . . you know. Breaks,' Catherine finished lamely.

Lilith snapped her head sideways like a velociraptor that's about to make your day so much worse. 'Certainly,' she said.

Apparently Catherine hadn't noticed the sarcasm iceberg that was heading her way. 'Oh, that's wonderful,' she gushed. 'Should I talk to your assistant about a budget, or –'

Lilith interrupted her. 'How about a soft play area, too?'

'Soft . . . play area?'

'Yes,' said Lilith, warming to her theme. 'Lots of lovely soft blocks for you all to play with. Oh, I know! We could install a candy-floss vending machine, too. And how about a roller coaster? You know what, why don't we all just come to work dressed as clowns? We can park our clown cars in the car park, flollop into the laboratory in our oversized clown shoes, and spend the day squirting each other with water from novelty flowers in the lapels of our clown jackets. Would you like that, er, Catherine?'

Catherine was already backing away towards the lift. 'No, no, that's fine,' she said, becoming increasingly alarmed at the fury in Lilith's heavy-lidded, red-rimmed eyes. *It looks like she hasn't slept for a week,* she thought to herself. *No, scratch that. It looks like she hasn't been to sleep . . . ever.* 'Sorry to bother you,' she soothed, holding up her hands as if placating an enraged buffalo, while jabbing frantically at the lift buttons with an outstretched elbow. 'I'll get back to work, then. Bye!'

The lift doors slid closed. Lilith gave a frustrated harrumphing noise and slumped back in her chair. The white room swam in front of her exhausted eyes and, just for a moment, she allowed them to close.

'Things have gone downhill around here,' said a thin, vinegary voice from behind her. Lilith jerked round to see her father's portrait raising its grizzled eyebrows and looking at her disdainfully. 'In my day, members of staff would never have marched into the chief executive's office, demanding coffee machines and I don't know what. They wouldn't have dreamed of it.'

'Dreamed,' muttered Lilith, realizing with a shock that she had fallen asleep in her chair. 'I'm dreaming.' Panic fluttered inside her like a trapped bird. Sleeping was the thing she hated most – the only time she was off guard. The time when her horrible father invaded her dreams and there was no possibility of escape until she woke up.

'You're a sad disappointment, Lilith,' said her father's painting acidly.

Lilith struggled desperately to wake, like a swimmer flailing frantically towards the surface. **'Shut up!'** she spat.

'Shut . . . UP!'

Her eyes flew open.

'I haven't actually said anything yet,' replied the whiny voice of a man who'd come out of the lift while she'd been asleep. 'But I shall remain shut up until told otherwise, sir!'

Lilith rubbed her eyes with the heels of her hands. She was completely and utterly exhausted. But staying awake was the only way to avoid her father's hectoring voice. Until her invention was ready, that is. Soon she would be able to sleep peacefully, she thought to herself. It was vital that nothing went wrong. She blinked, digging her nails into the palms of her hands to goad herself into alertness. 'General Pheare,' she said. 'Thank you for coming.'

The man standing in front of her desk was short and plump, dressed in a dark suit that looked too big for him. His large, bulbous head was topped by only a few strands of wispy hair, but his face was small and mean-looking, crammed into the middle of the huge head like a child's drawing on a dangerously over-inflated balloon. It looked as if someone had ordered a head in extra-large, but accidentally ordered extra-extra-small features to go on the front of it. A phone headset was plugged into one ear, with a curly wire disappearing among the folds of his neck into his white shirt. He was, of course, the very same man Maya had seen from the hospital window.

'Thank you for coming, General Pheare,' repeated Lilith, puzzled as to why the little man hadn't responded.

Pheare said nothing, clamping his lips together and rocking forward on to the balls of his feet a couple of times.

'You can cease shutting up,' said Lilith, realizing what was going on. 'I wasn't talking to you, anyway. I was telling my . . . never mind.'

'Sir! YES, SIR!'

snapped Pheare, his sleeve flapping as he pressed a small moist hand to the enormous expanse of his forehead in salute. General Pheare was the head of security at Somnia Incorporated. He had been appointed by Lilith's mean old father, and given a huge amount of money to set up what was, in effect, his own private army. But it's important to point out that he was not, in fact, a general. His actual name had been Gordon Pheare, but he'd legally changed it to General Gordon Pheare. That alone should tell you everything you need to know about him.

'General,' began Lilith, who had known him since she was little, so was on first-name terms, 'I've called you here this morning for a very important purpose.'

73

This was not a surprise to General Pheare. Staff hardly ever got called to Lilith Delamere's office, reached only by its private lift. If you got summoned there, it usually meant something incredibly bad was about to happen.

'I have some very exciting news,' she continued. 'For your ears only, of course.'

Pheare nodded curtly. He thought of himself as a cross between a crack military strategist and an international spy, so this kind of talk was music to his ears. Unfortunately he wasn't actually a cross between those two things. He was a cross between a somewhat dim little round man, and an even dimmer little round man. But, hey, you've got to admire his confidence, right?

'Finally, after years of work, I am close to a major breakthrough,' Lilith went on, leaning across the desk, her exhausted eyes lighting up with a strange, pale light. 'My research is about to come to fruition. Somnia is about to quite literally change the world.'

'Change the world.' Pheare nodded again. 'Right. Excellent. Understood.'

'And, that being the case,' said Lilith, 'it is absolutely

imperative that we tighten up security. Anything and anyone that threatens my plan must be wiped out. Ruthlessly. I'm giving you *carte blanche*. Do I make myself clear?'

'Crystalline,' replied Pheare, with more relish than an over-garnished cheeseburger. 'Ruthlessly wiped out. Got it. And, yes, great news about the new addition. French, is she?'

Lilith's forehead pursed like a freshly salted slug. 'French? What on earth are you talking about?'

'The new – you know . . . the new operative you mentioned. Blanche. I assumed she must be French. Maybe not French. Canadian, perhaps. Or possibly just one of her grandparents . . .'

'Will you stop blithering!' rapped out Lilith. Pheare sprang to attention. 'Have you no idea what *carte blanche* means?'

'Not a French lady, then?' asked General Pheare. He was the sort of man who would never admit he was wrong, but he'd kind of been backed into a corner on this one.

'It means,' said Lilith, quietly and viciously, 'that I

am authorizing you to use any means necessary to keep this project safe. Additional security, additional staff. Any means necessary. Do we understand each other?'

'Oh yes, indeed,' replied Pheare, his fish-like little eyes gleaming.

'Keep a special eye on Clayton,' warned Lilith. 'When we visited the hospital yesterday . . . I don't know. Something made me uneasy.'

'We've got guards at the hospital, sir,' protested Pheare. 'I inspected them personally during our visit.'

'Double them,' instructed Lilith. 'Double them.'

'You mean, quadruple them?'

Lilith shot him a look that would have made an icicle shiver. 'What?'

'You said to double them twice,' said Pheare, 'so did you mean –'

'Whatever guards there are,' said Lilith slowly and furiously, **'DOUBLE THEM.'**

'And is that in addition to your previous announcement? Because that would mean, er –' he searched for the right word and failed to find it –

'octupulizing them.'

'Listen to me very carefully,' said Lilith, rubbing her exhausted eyes. 'Forget the previous exchange. The level of guards at the hospital when you entered this room, yes? I would like that number to be doubled.'

'Sah!' Pheare stamped to attention, one of his shoes coming off in the process. One other thing we should tell you about him is that he was extremely embarrassed at being so small. This explains why his clothes and shoes were always a few sizes too big – he was too proud to tell shop assistants his actual measurements.

Lilith watched him as he tried to subtly put his shoe back on while remaining at attention, almost overbalancing in the process. Pheare was an extremely irritating person – but he was efficient and completely ruthless. And there was no room in her plans for even the slightest hint of ruth. 'Most of all,' she told him firmly, 'watch the daughter. Maya. There's something I don't trust about her.'

'We're watching her, too,' Pheare insisted. 'Got someone outside her house day and night. She knows nothing. And even if she did suspect anything . . . what could she possibly do about it?'

'I don't know,' admitted Lilith reluctantly. 'But she's a determined little thing.'

'Misses her daddy,' said Pheare in his reedy voice. 'Well, we can understand that, can't we? I mean, when your father was in charge here –'

'That will be all, General,' snapped Lilith abruptly. Pheare had hero-worshipped her father. His office was, in fact, decorated with photographs of himself and Doctor Damian Delamere in various chummy poses. The last thing she wanted, especially after yet another disturbing dream about her father, was a homily about what a fantastic, visionary boss he had been.

'Understood,' Pheare replied, saluting for absolutely no valid reason and about-turning. 'And don't worry about little Maya,' he said over his shoulder as he marched towards the lift. 'We'll keep her on a tight leash. There's no possible way she could ever be a threat.

HA!

One little girl taking on the might of Somnia and **Pheare's army!**

IN HER DREAMS! '

He gave a harsh laugh as the door closed, completely unaware of the dense cloud of irony he had just expelled like a stinky literary burp.

CHAPTER 4
THE DREAM BANDITS

That night, Maya waited till the strip of light under her bedroom door had blinked out, meaning her mum had gone to bed. She smoothed out the piece of paper on which she'd written Teddy's instructions, and read them through for the thirty-seventh time. Bin Bag, once again curled up in his customary spot at the end of her bed, blinked at her owlishly – though he was, we should point out, not an owl.

Maya's stomach churned with anxiety as she considered what she was about to do, but the thought of her dad kept her going. Was it actually possible that she might be able to talk to him? To rescue him? Even if it was a long shot, it was a shot worth taking.

As silently as a giraffe in the middle of a sponsored silence, Maya eased her bedroom window open and swung herself on to the ledge. The moonlit garden stretched away from her, criss-crossed with a lattice of shadows. She pushed herself off the window ledge and landed on the soft grass with a slight *whumph*.

Dropping into a ninja-esque crouch, she waited for a moment to make sure nobody had heard, before stalking round the side of the house and away.

Looking left and right up and down her street, Maya remembered Teddy's final instruction, and a cold finger of fear teased her back. *Make sure they're not following*, he had told her. *You're being watched.* She peered across at a car parked opposite her house. It was hard to tell in the dim light, but she was almost sure that a figure was sitting in the passenger seat. In the orangey glow of a street light she thought she caught a faint reflection, as if a face were turned towards her house. The words sounded in her head again:

'YOU'RE BEING WATCHED.'

Ducking behind a shrub, Maya dropped on to her tummy and started to wriggle away from the parked car like a well-drilled military worm. She was desperately trying to keep herself calm. Teddy had promised that everything would be properly explained when they met in person – and Maya was very much hoping that was the case. If it wasn't, she was growing rather concerned that her head might explode. But the thought of rescuing her dad kept her going as she reached the end of the road and, with one last glance backwards to check the car hadn't moved, she began to jog away, the fuzzy hood of her coat pulled right up for warmth and disguising purposes.

Round one more corner, Maya came to the bus stop where Teddy had told her to wait. The light in the bus shelter was broken and kept flickering on and off, but she sat down on the narrow red plastic seat. She thought she heard a low whistle, and a moment later there was a screeching of tyres from somewhere close by. Maya tensed, wondering if the car from outside her house was following her after all. But the vehicle that came careering round the corner a few seconds later was definitely not that car. It was bigger, scruffier, stranger, and infinitely cooler.

Turning so sharply that it actually tipped on to two wheels at one point, a large van screeched into the street. It was broad and squat, painted bright purple, with the words MATT'S MATTRESSES in garish orange letters along the side. Strangest of all, an enormous mattress was fixed to the top of the van on springs. Aside from the screeching of tyres, the van was largely silent – emitting only a low whine rather than the coughing of an old-fashioned engine.

With a final skid, it ground to a halt beside the bus stop and the passenger door was flung open.

Maya could see Teddy Flamewood beckoning urgently from the driver's seat. Leaping off the plastic bench, she peered past him to make sure there wasn't, in fact, an adult with him in the front of the van. There wasn't.

'Sure you weren't followed?' hissed Teddy urgently.

'How are you driving a van?' hissed Maya back at him. 'You're, like, fourteen years old.'

'I asked you first,' protested Teddy.

'OK, OK.' Maya held up her hands. 'Yes, I'm sure I wasn't followed. There's some guy in a car outside my house, but I gave him the slip.'

'Great work!' Teddy congratulated her. 'We'll make a secret agent of you yet! Quick, jump in!'

Looking up and down the deserted street, Maya scrambled into the van.

'Right – my question now, please,' she said, trying to shake an unnerving feeling that she was dreaming this whole thing. It's a fairly strange experience, being picked up in a bright purple van by a boy you've only ever seen previously when you were fast asleep. 'How are you driving a van?'

Teddy grinned at her. 'By pushing the pedals,' he replied smugly. 'It's easy, look!' He jammed his right foot forward and the van shot crazily away down the road, swerving to avoid some dustbins that had been left out beside the pavement, before swinging into a wide U-turn and speeding off in the direction it had come from.

'Not quite what I meant,' said Maya grimly, scrabbling for her seatbelt.

'Don't worry,' said a girl's voice from behind her. 'Teddy's incredibly annoying, but he's actually not a bad driver. And this is an emergency rescue mission, after all.'

Maya craned her neck to look into the back of the van, and immediately cried out in surprise.

The back of the Flamewoods' van

was without doubt the strangest back-of-a-van that Maya had ever seen. She didn't have huge experience of van backs, but we can officially confirm that it was actually the strangest back-of-a-van that *anybody* has ever seen.

Imagine a van that delivers parcels to your house. That's your conventional van.
Weirdness factor: **zero**.

Now imagine a van that serves as a bus service for bees. A bee bus, if you will. A busload of bees.
Weirdness factor: **four**.

Now imagine that it's driven by a giant bee.
Weirdness factor: **six**.

Well, the Flamewoods' van easily scored a **ten** on the weirdness factor scale that we've just made up.

THIS
IS WHAT
IT LOOKED
LIKE.

In the centre was a battered old armchair. It looked beaten-up and scuffed, but incredibly comfortable. The sort of chair that you're not allowed to sit in at your grandparents' house because it's the cosiest thing in the world and your granddad has an incredibly refreshing nap in it every day. The chair sat on a faded fluffy rug, which also looked like it came from your grandparents' house. But that was where the old-people theme ended. Each of the walls was lined with an incredible array of screens, control panels, circuit boards and wiring. And at the back, surrounded by a complex arrangement of screens, a girl sat on a hard metal chair. The inside of the van was only dimly lit, but Maya could see that she was smiling and waving – and that she was clearly Teddy's twin sister. It was as if someone had grabbed Teddy, cut his hair short and arranged it in a series of curls before putting a pair of large black-rimmed glasses on him.

'You must be Bea!' called Maya. The girl gave a thumbs up in reply, raising her eyebrows above alert, intelligent eyes.

'This must seem super-weird,' called Bea, steadying

her chair as Teddy threw the van round another corner. 'Don't worry – you'll know everything in a few minutes – promise. If Teddy doesn't crash on the way, that is.' She gave a friendly smile to indicate that this was a joke, but Maya couldn't help reaching out and double-checking her seatbelt.

'So what's with the mouldy old chair?' asked Maya, turning to face forward again. 'It looks like a theme park for moths back there.'

'Oi! That's the world's most comfortable piece of seating, I'll have you know!' complained Teddy. 'That's the NAP chair I told you about. Remember, we're rescuing him from a *dream*,' he went on. 'And you're not going to get inside a dream without a Nocturnal Access Portal – NAP. Get it?'

'Which I built, by way,' added Bea from the back. 'Teddy likes to pretend he's some kind of super-spy or something – but he wouldn't get very far without the technology to back him up.' She clambered out of her seat and made her way forward, past the comfortable chair. Maya twisted round to study it. Now her eyes were adjusting slightly to the low light in the back of the van – all the electrical panels and rows of lights were off – she could see that it wasn't just a worn-out chair in the middle of a rug. There were thick snakes of wiring leading underneath it, and some kind of complicated gadget attached to the back of the headrest. 'We'll explain it all when we get there,' Bea promised as she flipped down a small seat and smiled at Maya kindly. 'But I can try and answer any questions on the way.'

'On the way where, by the way?' Maya wanted to know. There had been several other questions jostling for position like horses ready to start a race, but this question-horse had been parachuted in at the last second.

'On the way to find your dad,' Bea replied, raising her eyebrows slightly in surprise. 'I thought Teddy had explained that much to you, at least.' She shot her twin brother a disapproving look.

'Teddy has a tendency to . . . how shall I put this?' Maya began.

'Get so carried away with being a smart-trousers that he doesn't actually tell you what you want to know?'

Bea suggested. 'Yeah, we know. You want to try living with him.'

'I'm not sure I do, actually,' said Maya. 'Anyway, where are we going?'

'As Teddy should have explained,' Bea told her, 'your father is trapped inside a dream. We've been trying to locate him.'

'We call ourselves

THE DREAM BANDITS,'

said Teddy proudly.

'Teddy calls us the Dream Bandits,' Bea corrected. 'And he's still hoping it'll catch on.'

'So, Dream Bandits,' said Maya, testing it out and discovering that it did sound kind of exciting, 'how do we rescue my dad?'

'We thought we'd be able to do it without involving you,' Bea told her. 'We know which dream he's inside.'

'There's a problem, though,' continued Teddy, as he pulled the van to a quiet halt beside a high brick wall that Maya immediately recognized as the one surrounding Hagstone Court hospital. 'We can't find him.'

*

'So . . . tell me again about the chair – the Nocturnal Access Portal?' Maya asked Teddy uncertainly a few minutes later. They had climbed over the seats into the back of the van and Maya was regarding the comfortable, battered old armchair with a doubtful expression.

Bea broke in. 'Again, it's more of a show-and-tell situation. We can try and explain for ages – but once you see this for yourself, you'll appreciate just what your dad has invented. And why it has put him in so much danger.'

'OK.' Maya gave a small, determined nod and sat down. 'Woah,' she exclaimed immediately as she leaned back, 'this really is the most comfortable piece of seating ever.' It felt like the NAP chair was giving her a giant hug, but she quickly remembered the thick snakes of wiring and the control panels. This was no ordinary item of furniture.

'Told you.' Teddy laughed, reaching behind Maya's head. 'Now – have you ever seen old ladies at the hairdresser's, underneath those massive big dryer things?'

'Er, yeah,' said Maya uncertainly.

'Well . . . this is gonna be like sitting under one of those, without a copy of *Lady Time* magazine or whatever it's called.' He pulled forward, and Maya's vision dimmed as something descended over her head. Craning her neck, she looked upward to see that it was a dome made of a dark smoky plastic.

'This is exactly like one of those things at the hairdresser's,' she told Teddy. Then she noticed a small sticky label on the dome's lower edge reading PROPERTY OF KRAZY KUTTS. 'Hang on,' she corrected herself, 'this actually *is* one of those things at the hairdresser's.'

'Ah, yeah,' admitted Bea in an embarrassed tone. 'The real Dream Dome that your dad and our mum have been working on is a lot more high-tech. We had to improvise this from her plans.'

'I found that in a skip!' broke in Teddy proudly, 'and once we cleaned all the smears of blue hair dye off, it works great!'

'Ignore him,' Bea soothed. 'This is actually a fully functioning dream portal, I promise.'

Maya, still examining the dome, could now make out

a pair of speakers on either side. And set into the plastic in front of her like a jewel in an elaborate crown was a golden egg-shaped device. 'What's that?' Maya wanted to know.

'That,' Bea explained, 'is your father's incredible invention. The Clayton Hypnagogic Energy-Enhancing Sensor Ellipse.'

'So . . . CHEESE for short,' Maya observed.

'Told you she was smart,' said Teddy.

Maya blushed slightly and looked more closely at the egg-shaped device. It was made of glass, and inside she could see a series of thin transparent wires and what looked like tiny light bulbs. Beside it was a strip of red sticky label reading SHIELD EYES FROM LIGHT.

'The Sensor Ellipse is what connects you to the Hypnagogic Field,' Bea went on.

'The hypno . . . goggles . . . what now?'

Bea gave a small laugh. 'Hypnagogic,' she corrected. 'It's a field of energy created by everyone's dreams. Your dad's a genius – this device patches you into the field.'

'Hold on a minute,' said Maya. 'Are you telling me

that my dad invented something called CHEESE – that makes you have really vivid dreams?'

'Oh yeah,' said Teddy. 'Never thought of it like that.'

'That's the most my-dad thing ever,' said Maya, missing him even more. She could imagine the smile on his face when he named his invention.

'Anyway, like I said, it's easier to show you than try and explain it,' said Bea, flicking a switch in front of her. Suddenly Maya heard Bea's voice coming through the speakers on either side of the plastic dome. 'Ready to back-watch,' Bea declared.

'Bea will monitor you,' Teddy explained, 'and she can use the dome to pull you out if she needs to.'

'This isn't going to hurt, is it?' Maya was growing slightly alarmed.

'Of course not,' soothed Teddy. 'It's a slightly odd feeling, though, entering the Dream Field. You know that sensation you sometimes get when you're just about to drop off – the falling one?'

'Yeeeeees,' said Maya.

'You might get that. Only . . . a bit more. Just go with it. It'll pass. Bea – she's ready. Activate.'

'Activate,' repeated Bea's voice in Maya's ears. There was a small beep and immediately the egg-shaped device began to pulse with golden light, which rapidly filled the whole dome. At the same time, Maya's body was flooded with a warm, comfortable sensation. It felt like snuggling down under the thickest possible duvet after the coldest possible day, knowing there's no school the next morning. Oh, and you're wearing the cosiest possible pair of socks. Unless you hate sleeping in socks, in which case discount that part. In fact, discount that part anyway. We've just realized that sleeping in socks is the worst thing in the world ever.

'Sweet dreams,' Maya heard Teddy say – as if from a long distance away.

'Stop being creepy, Teddy,' came Bea's voice in the speakers. 'You squealed like a baby pig the first time you did this. Here you go, Maya. Remember . . . just relax.'

Bathed in the warm golden glow, Maya had felt far too warm and comfortable to take much notice. But suddenly everything changed. The golden light and the inside of the van vanished – and she had the sickening sensation of falling. She remembered a roller coaster she'd once been on with her mum, which had paused at the top of its track before

plunging them downwards.

This felt like that – only in a comfier chair and without a kid being sick in the seat behind you, which is what had happened at the theme park.

'Not loving this,' said Maya through gritted teeth, gripping the arms of the chair as she felt herself falling faster and faster.

'Almost there,' Bea's calm voice reassured her. 'You're doing great, not making any piglet noises at all, unlike my useless brother.'

Maya *was* growing fairly tempted to start making some kind of high-pitched noise. But, abruptly, just as the falling sensation was becoming unbearable, it stopped.

Maya collected herself and looked around. At first the light was too dazzling to see very far. Her body felt a little peculiar, as though it was lighter than usual.

The thing she noticed first of all was the temperature. It wasn't cold, it wasn't warm. It was . . . perfect. Maya found herself remembering a time when she'd felt something similar. She'd been on holiday with her mum and dad in a hot country, and they'd had to get up early to catch a small ferry to a different island. She remembered standing on the dock with the dawn just breaking over the ocean. The heat of the day had not yet begun to build, and the breeze coming in off the sea felt like silk against her skin. That was what it felt like in this dream space – the most perfect temperature imaginable.

A slight movement caught her eye and she looked down in surprise to see a large black shape beside her in the brilliant white light. A furry, dishevelled shape. It was her cat, Bin Bag.

'What on earth are you doing here?' she asked out loud, without thinking.

'I was about to ask you the exact same question,' replied Bin Bag in exactly the sort of voice she'd always imagined he would have. It was deep, cultured and – there was no better word for it – rather catty.

'**WHOAH,**' said Maya in astonishment. '**I can talk to CATS!**'

'Anyone can talk to cats.' Bin Bag sniffed dismissively. 'People talk to cats all the time. It's getting cats to talk back to you that's really impressive.'

Maya thought about this for a moment. 'Fair point,' she conceded.

'Who are you talking to?' came a disembodied voice through the clouds of bright white.

'Bea? Is that you?' asked Maya.

'Yeah,' confirmed Bea. 'I've got you on the dream monitor. Wait for a moment and things will get easier to see. But who's that with you?'

'It's . . . um, my cat, actually,' Maya replied, feeling a little embarrassed.

'O . . . K,' said Bea's uncertain voice. 'That's certainly new. Ask your dad about it, he's the expert.'

Maya's heart gave a leap. Was it really possible that she was about to see her father? To talk to him? After six whole weeks sitting by his bed in hospital?

'Relax,' said Bin Bag, as if reading her thoughts. 'Getting all panicky won't help anyone. You need to be more cat about this.'

'You run away from squirrels,' Maya reminded him sternly.

'Those things are psychotic,' Bin Bag protested. 'You'd run away too if you were my size.'

Now that Maya's eyes had started to adjust to the dazzling white light, she could see her surroundings more clearly. She was standing in a wide, circular white space. Several large pictures in ornate golden frames hung on the wall – but the pictures were moving. The one directly ahead of Maya showed a mouse riding a cat, like a cowboy on a horse, waving its little mouse hat in the air.

'Welcome to the Zoetrope,' said Bea's disembodied voice.

'Cowboy mouse,' gabbled Maya, 'horse cat.'

'Ah, yes, that's a weird one, isn't it?' Bea replied. 'That – let me check . . .' Maya could hear the clicking of a keyboard for a few moments. 'That is a dream currently being experienced by Mr Graham Todd, who is a librarian living in . . .' More tapping of computer keys. 'In that house just across the street. Wonderful imaginations, librarians.'

Maya looked around at some of the other pictures. Some of the other *dreams*, she mentally corrected herself. The wall, she now realized, was rotating slowly, giving the sensation of being on the world's slowest and most surreal merry-go-round. One frame showed an image of clouds – clearly someone was dreaming about flying. Another showed a faint, fuzzy image of a packed stadium with a chubby man waving to the cheering crowds from the top of a podium as an official placed a gold medal round his neck. 'Roland Brown,' Bea's voice broke in. 'Took up jogging two weeks ago. He's had this dream five times since then. His house is a bit further away, so that one's trickier to see.'

'This is amazing,' breathed Maya. 'You can actually watch people's dreams.'

'You can do more than watch them,' corrected Bea. 'You can walk right into them, remember? And, yes, it is amazing. Your dad's a clever guy.'

Maya felt a warm surge of pride and looked down to share it with Bin Bag, but he had lain down nearby and was washing his paws with a disinterested air.

'So where is he?' she asked, looking around in confusion.

Bin Bag got up and wandered away, crouching in front of the picture of the mouse riding the cat, whipping the end of his tail from side to side. 'That's not helping, by the way,' Maya told him. She looked at the gently rotating walls. Which of the dreams was the

one where Lilith had trapped the professor?

She felt a sudden gust of chilly air on the side of her neck and turned her head. One of the pictures was darker than the others. Inside the frame she could only make out dark grey stone walls fading into blackness. A carved stone plaque above it showed the number VII.

'Dream Seven,' came Bea's disembodied voice. 'That's where he's been trapped. Well, I say dream . . .'

'It's a nightmare, isn't it?' asked Maya, walking over and standing in front of the picture. Bin Bag gave up stalking his cowboy mouse and came to join her, the cold breeze flowing from Dream Seven rippling his scruffy black fur.

'That's where your father is,' Bea's voice confirmed. 'Trouble is . . . we can't find him in there. Every time we go in, it's just a passageway leading us in a circle. We need to get an exact fix on his location within the dream to have a chance of pulling him out, but it's like a maze in there.'

'And you think I can find him?' Maya squared her shoulders, peering into the dank stone passageway. It seemed to play tricks with her eyes, telescoping off into the black distance. And something prickled at the very edges of her hearing –

A FAINT AND UNDENIABLY CREEPY WHISPERING.

'It's your dad's dream,' Bea replied. 'If anyone can track him down in there, it's got to be you. Maybe you know things about him that will give you clues. Things he's scared of, things he's said to you. It's our best chance, anyway.'

Maya shivered and reached down to ruffle Bin Bag's fur for comfort.

'It'll be fine,' the cat told her, although she had to admit he sounded less than completely convinced. 'Sinister dark passageway straight out of a grown man's nightmares. What could possibly go wrong?'

'Don't worry,' echoed Bea's voice in her head. 'If it gets too scary in there, we can pull you straight out again.'

'You won't need to,' said Maya determinedly. 'I'm going to find him.' And before she could think about it too carefully, she stepped forward, straight into the dream. Bin Bag followed, slinking through the picture frame with a brief mew of doubt, which we'd like you to try out loud now . . .

EXCELLENT.

CHAPTER 5
DEXTER'S DREAM

Walking from the Zoetrope into her father's nightmare felt like slipping into an unheated swimming pool in mid February. In other words, extremely unpleasant. Maya felt a slight resistance as she entered the dream, almost like the surface tension of water. But when she pushed through, the chilly air closed behind her. A sudden fluttering of panic beat around her brain like bats' wings, but she silenced it sternly.

This was a **RESCUE MISSION.**

There was **NO TIME** for **PANIC.**

She looked ahead down the stone passageway, trying to work out what it was that made the whole scene look so extremely odd. It took her a few moments, but once she realized, her brain reeled.

The passage was long, lined with narrow, high, arched windows of the kind you find in a castle. But there was something deeply unsettling about the light. Because instead of light flowing in through the arches, there was darkness. The stone walls and paving stones underfoot were glowing with a very soft, pale radiance. But the windows cast dark shadows across them as thick night streamed in. Frowning, Maya waved her hand in front of the first window on her left. Instead of her hand casting a shadow on the opposite wall, she could see a silvery echo of her hand as it blocked the dark.

'It's really very unpleasant in here,' Bin Bag pointed out. 'Not my scene at all. Even slightly.'

'Thanks for your support,' Maya snapped at him. The place was making her edgy.

'If you wanted bravery and faithfulness, you should have got a dog,' he replied.

'Well, could you at least try to be a bit more dog?'

pleaded Maya. Suddenly the thought of a large dog trotting alongside her felt comforting.

'That,' Bin Bag replied, 'is the most insulting thing I have ever heard. Anyway, come on. Let's find the professor and get out of here.'

'All right,' agreed Maya, beginning to edge gingerly down the passageway. The shadow streaming in through the windows felt oddly thick and hard to move through. And the whispering was growing louder. She had the unnerving impression that it was saying something about *her*, even though it was far too faint to make out any actual words. And what was even worse was the creeping, rootless feeling that she was being followed. Shaking her head to try and clear it, she glanced once over her shoulder and walked on, picking up her pace.

Her footsteps slapped eerily on the cold stone floor as she padded onward,

following
bends in
the passageway –

first to the RIGHT,

then to the LEFT,

then TWICE to the RIGHT again.

And all the time, that strange sensation kept on growing – a tantalizing tickle on the back of her neck that constantly threatened to transform into an overwhelming desire to start running. The thought that they were being followed by something just out of sight began to fill Maya's brain as she and Bin Bag hurried round yet more bends in the stone corridor, patches of pale, glowing stone and inky blackness flashing past them as they walked faster and faster.

'You know, I'm convinced we're just going round in a circle,' said Bin Bag after a while. 'I'm sure I've seen that stone before. At least twice.'

'Which stone?' Maya asked him in a small, scared voice. 'All the stones look the same.'

'That one, over there,' Bin Bag replied, lifting a paw

and pointing. Maya couldn't see anything different about it. But as she peered at it, something caught the corner of her eye. A flash of movement in the darkness behind them.

'There's something there,' Maya wailed, finally giving into the panic that had been circling her like a cloud of choking black smoke.

'RUN!'

Together they began to sprint along the stone floor.

'Maya! Maya! Are you OK? Do you need me to pull you out?' she could hear Bea calling.

'No! This is the only chance to find my dad!' she replied out loud. And, inwardly, she began to scold herself for giving in to fear: *Think, Maya Clayton, think. It's just a nightmare. What do we know about nightmares? I'm sure there was something* . . . She actually knocked a fist on the side of her head in frustration as she ran. *What did Dad tell me – years ago?*

And suddenly, she remembered.

The memory was sketchy and faint – it must have happened when she was very, very young. As if she were watching a damaged piece of film from years and years ago, Maya saw herself sitting up in a small bed, with her dad perched on the side of it, his hand on her forehead. She'd been having a series of bad dreams, she remembered. Dreams about being chased . . .

'There's nothing to worry about.' She heard her father's voice echoing back to her from long ago. 'It's just a bad dream.'

'But there was a monster, Dad! A monster was chasing me!'

'Was it definitely chasing you?' the professor mused, smiling. 'I've studied dreams a lot, you know, Maya. And do you know what I think? I think that if there's a monster in your dream, the chances are that it just wants to talk to you.' He pulled the duvet up round her neck and tucked her in as he continued: 'Perhaps it has something to tell you – or something *you* need to tell *it*. So if it's chasing you . . . well, you chase it right back!'

'WAOW!

What on earth do you think you're doing?' wailed Bin Bag as Maya stopped mid stride and spun round in the cold stone passageway. 'I thought we were being chased round in circles through a creepy castle by a scary monster!'

'Nope,' Maya corrected him. 'If there's a monster in your dream – well, chances are that it just wants to tell you something. So now it's *us* doing the chasing.' And she began to dash back in the opposite direction.

Now she had turned the tables, Maya could dimly make out the large hulking shape that had been chasing her. It was off-white and shaggy, and almost filled the stone corridor. But as soon as she turned and began to pursue it, it started shambling off in the other direction at a surprisingly fast pace.

Another strange thing happened after Maya turned round. The impression that they were simply going round in circles disappeared. Instead of the same stretches of dim stone tunnel ahead of her, the passageway began to change, growing wider in places with larger windows.

After a while, they began to run past junctions, where other corridors branched off. Each time Maya had to stop and strain her eyes to see where her quarry had gone, but always the faint, faraway sight of the pale, shaggy shape told her which way to go.

'I have the distinct impression that we're starting to go downhill,' panted Bin Bag, galloping along beside her as fast as his furry legs would carry him. And Maya realized this was true – the widening and curving passageways had begun to **SLOPE DOWNWARDS,**

making their progress slightly easier. The darkness pouring in through the windows was fading, too.

Once or twice Maya caught a glimpse of a view out of some of the archways, but there was no time to stop. She was convinced that the creature ahead of them was leading them in the right direction. **She mustn't let it GET AWAY.**

'Maya, what's going on?' sounded Bea's voice. 'Are you still going in circles?'

'No,' she replied, panting. 'You only go round in circles if you're running away. Once you turn round it's easier.'

'What?' came the baffled reply. But there was no time to stop and explain. There would be plenty of time for that later. By now the passageway was far wider and brighter – the bone-chilling cold had vanished, and instead of darkness flowing through the stone windows, there was a quite noticeable, pale, pre-dawn kind of daylight. Faint patches of green flashed at the edges of Maya's vision as she urged her exhausted legs to keep going. The gigantic pale shape was still dimly visible ahead of her, lumbering along in the gloom, until it turned one last corner and ducked out of sight. Maya broke into a final, lung-igniting sprint and hurled herself to her right to follow it. Here, at last, she found the forbidding stone walls had disappeared.

Maya and Bin Bag stumbled through a large archway into a moss-covered courtyard filled with tall pine trees and their barky, resinous scent. The air was still cool but the cold was no longer oppressive. The ground beneath her feet was soft and yielding as she stepped gingerly towards the centre of the courtyard, casting nervous glances to either side for the hulking shape that she had just chased here.

'Dad?' she called out hesitantly into the dawn light. 'Dad . . . are you here? Hello?'

'Hey, Scribbles,' came a quiet, kind voice from somewhere behind her.

Maya turned to see her father walking towards her through the trees. He looked healthy and – crucially – wide awake. Even more important, his thin round glasses were once more balanced on his nose, and his long stripy scarf was wound round his neck. Tears sprang to her eyes as she saw the walking, talking, scarf-wearing Dad she knew and loved. It hit her once again how upsetting it had been to see him lying in bed with those trademark accessories folded up on the table beside him. And the sound of the nickname that he alone used brought it home to her: she had done it – she had found him! Maya ran forward and hugged him tightly.

'Good day, Professor Dexter,' said Bin Bag, who had sat down on a tree stump to avoid getting his paws dirty on the mossy forest floor.

'Hello, Bin Bag,' said the professor, before releasing Maya from their hug and performing a very impressive double take. **'WHOAH, hang on.**

How come you've brought THE CAT with you?'

'It's not that I brought him,' explained Maya. 'I found him here waiting for me. When I got into that dreamy weird room – the zoo . . . zoo . . . whatever you call it.'

'Zoetrope?'

'Right. Well, there he was. And he can talk.'

'I think he might have worked that part out for himself,' Bin Bag pointed out, flicking his tail.

Professor Dexter squatted down on his haunches to stare at the cat, who stared right back with his knowing green eyes. 'But this is fascinating!' the professor exclaimed. 'You've actually managed to manifest yourself a companion, within someone else's dream!' He adjusted his glasses and reached out to tickle Bin

Bag behind the ear, still gazing at him in fascination. 'That's pretty advanced dreaming, you know.'

'I just, you know, looked down and there he was,' said Maya, feeling confused and a little embarrassed.

Her father got to his feet and grasped her by the shoulders. 'I've known it since you were small,' he told her. 'Your imagination really is something very special.'

'I never realized it would actually come in useful, though,' she replied.

'What could be more useful?' cried the professor. 'You've always kept plenty of space in your head for dreams – and here's the evidence!' He looked at her proudly, his wide grin lighting her up inside like a beacon. 'Your imagination is able to use the Dream Field as a . . . as a blank canvas! You were feeling scared and unsure, and your own mind supplied you with a comforting companion. An imaginary cat!'

'Imaginary?' echoed Bin Bag in a scandalized tone of voice.

'Don't feel bad,' reassured the professor. 'I can't think of anything finer than being imaginary.'

'You're a brain cat,' Maya told Bin Bag.

'I can't help feeling that being part of your brain does make me somewhat less impressive,' said the cat and sniffed. 'But we need to play the cards we're dealt, I suppose.' And with that, he curled up facing away from them and appeared to go to sleep.

'So, Dad,' said Maya, questions tumbling over themselves in a rush to get out of her brain,

'what on earth is going on here?

What is this **DREAM FIELD**?

Where have you been
for the last six weeks?

And can we really **RESCUE YOU?**'

'I'll answer your last question first,' said the professor with a grin, 'because it has the shortest answer, which is yes – at least, I hope so.'

'Seriously?' Hope surged in Maya's chest like a swelling tide.

'But to explain how, I'll need to answer your first two questions – and that might take a few more minutes. Shall we sit?' He gestured towards a fallen tree nearby, at convenient sitting height, and together they perched themselves on the trunk.

'I can't pretend to know everything about the Hypnagogic Field,' Maya's father began, 'or the Dream Field, as you called it. I suspected its existence for many years before I managed to actually get inside. It's an area of energy created by all the dreaming people around the world. A kind of collective imagination, if you like.'

'So . . .' Maya looked around at the tranquil courtyard, 'we're kind of . . . inside your head right now? You've got a castle in your head?'

'We've all got castles in our heads,' said the professor, looking around with a wonderstruck expression, 'and everything that goes with them. Creepy passageways, tranquil courtyards, throne rooms, dungeons . . . The human imagination is truly wonderful. And it's only when we're asleep that we can get a proper look at them. When they're awake, humans tend to make a lot of pretty unpleasant things, don't they? But when they're asleep . . . all the ambition, and desire to impress, and paranoia, goes out of the window. This is what humanity's collective imagination actually looks like. And that gives me a lot of hope.' Maya was startled to see that tears had come into his eyes.

'And you invented a way to get inside this . . . this hypno—'

'Hypnagogic Field? Right. I tried for years, but last year I actually succeeded. And that's where Lilith Delamere comes in.'

'She's been checking up on you in hospital, you know,' Maya blurted out.

Professor Dexter looked serious. 'I'm not surprised. I know what she's planning to use my invention for, you see. And when I warned her I wouldn't let it happen, she trapped me in here.'

Maya thought back with fury to Lilith bending over her father's sleeping form in his hospital bed. 'So it's true, then,' she said grimly. 'Lilith trapped you. But what about the accident?'

'Oh, come on,' said Bin Bag, who, it seemed, was

only pretending to be asleep. 'There obviously wasn't really an accident at the laboratory.'

'Your imaginary cat is correct,' agreed Maya's father, 'which is to say, *you* are absolutely correct. Well done.'

'So . . . what did Lilith do to you?'

'Ah.' Her father held up a professorial finger. 'That is an interesting story . . .'

CHAPTER 6
THE INVENTION
OF CHEESE

It's time for a flashback, so let's all sing the flashback song together. You can make up any tune you like for it, but you must sing it out loud, otherwise you will dream boring dreams about a man in a suit called Iain reading his tax return out loud for an entire week.

READY?

Welllll, the plot of a book, it goes clickety clack,

As it rattles along like a train on a track.

But what might have happened before things had begun?

Are there bits of the story before Chapter One?

There might be a reason two things will connect,

But the authors withheld it for dramatic effect,

Or a reason a character's being a git,

And it all becomes clear when you skip back a bit.

And that's a flashback!

Whoa whoa whoa whoa.

Flashback! Flashington floo.

We need a flashback!

Zooming into the past,

Like a literary Doctor Who.

(Guitar solo)

Wasn't that REFRESHING?

Time for verse two. You've got to make up a completely different tune for this one.

Flashington flash, flashington flashback,
Wom pom piddle ding doo —

SQUAWK.

Hello. Apologies for the interruption. It's the Chief Puffin here, the head of Puffin Books. I normally live in a rabbit hole on a remote clifftop, which is where I run my publishing empire. But I just need to make a quick appearance in this book to deliver a message to my authors.

GET ON WITH THE STORY, YOU PAIR OF COMPLETE IDIOTS.

Thank you. I shall now return to my hole by flapping my unusually small wings.

SQUAWK.

CRIKEY,

that Chief Puffin's intimidating, isn't she?

Apologies, Your Royal Highness.
We got a bit distracted there.

OK, forget verse two of the song.

On with the flashback.

ONE YEAR AGO

'And you're absolutely certain this works?' Lilith Delamere was trembling with barely suppressed excitement as she followed Professor Dexter Clayton down the long passageway.

'It does indeed,' Dexter told her, smiling with pride. 'You're not going to believe it. It's so, so beautiful. Just incredible. Wait till you see.' He tapped a series of numbers into a keypad at the end of the corridor, and a thick steel door slid open.

Lilith had been in the central laboratory at Somnia many times, of course. But she had never seen it empty before. Normally during the daytime it was packed with technicians, scientists and engineers, working like bees on Somnia Incorporated's main project. But as soon as Professor Dexter had revealed that he had, for the first time, actually managed to enter a dream, she had instructed him to wait until the rest of the staff had gone for lunch in order to show her.

In the centre of the enormous room was a single metal chair, surrounded by a bewildering network of tubes, pipes and wiring. Suspended above it was a dome made of shiny polished metal, and on the front of the dome was an egg-shaped glass device, pulsing gently with a soft golden light. The walls of the huge room were lined with computers on desks and banks of monitors. It looked rather like a mad scientist's laboratory, and for a perfectly good reason – it was.

'You've actually managed to tap into the Hypnagogic Field? It really exists?' badgered Lilith as the professor led her to the chair.

'It certainly does,' he confirmed. 'Want to take a look?' He glanced at Lilith. Never, he thought to himself, had someone looked more in need of a good snooze. Her eyes were ringed with dark circles, but they were blazing with enthusiasm.

Hungrily, Lilith threw herself into the chair. 'Show me,' she demanded.

'With the very greatest pleasure.' The professor moved over to the largest bank of computer equipment and began tapping at two keyboards simultaneously. With a whine, the brightly polished dome descended until it enveloped Lilith's head.

'I finally got the CHEESE working,' the professor explained. 'The Clayton Hypnagogic Energy-Enhancing Sensor Ellipse. I'd been wondering for weeks why I couldn't stabilize the technology long enough to enter a dream and then, **WHAM!'**

'What, you had an idea?'

'No, I hit my head on the doorway. And *then* I had an idea. I suddenly realized how to reconfigure the circuitry to access the Hypnagogic Field. I tried it out while everyone was at lunch . . . and it worked!'

'You were actually able to see people's dreams?'

'I was. Not that many, of course, because, hey, it's lunchtime. And, you know, most people are awake, eating . . . er, their lunch . . . and stuff. But there must have been a couple of people who'd fallen asleep not far from here.'

Lilith fumed at the thought that those sleeping people might be working for her company. She wasn't paying her staff to sleep on the job. But then she realized – she now had the technology to catch them in the act! 'Show me,' she demanded a second time.

'Stand by . . .' Professor Dexter tapped more numbers into the keyboards. 'Prepare yourself, Ms Delamere. You are about to take a journey into dreams.'

'Only good ones, though, surely?' Lilith began to protest, suddenly terrified she was about to meet her father, as she did every night. But the dome round her head was already filling with a bright light and, before she knew what was happening, she was falling – just as Maya would do in the mattress van months later –

FALLING . . .

FALLING,

JOLT, she landed in a circle of white mist.

Lilith collected herself more quickly than Maya would do – but that shouldn't be a surprise. She was a collected kind of person. However, she wasn't accompanied by an imaginary talking cat, so we think we know who the overall winner is here.

She looked around, peering into the white clouds. A couple of indistinct shapes formed, one to the left and one to the right.

'I'll be able to refine all this,' she heard the voice of Professor Dexter say. 'Make it look like a room, you know – a cool art gallery or something. This is just a prototype.'

'So . . . what are those shapes I can see? Are those really . . . dreams?'

'Exactly. Two real, bona fide, live, direct dreams, happening right now, not far from here.'

'So, you can only access dreams nearby?'

'At the moment, yes. With more research I should be able to increase the range. But at the moment you need to be relatively close to the dreamer to access their part of the field.'

Lilith was walking towards one of the shapes in the blankness. 'So, I can just step inside?'

'The field brings all dreams together. And, at the moment, thanks to my – ahem – rather incredible invention, your waking mind is a part of that field. So, yes, you can go anywhere you like.'

Lilith stepped forward, her face stern and set.

Kevin Hopper was a hard worker. He was one of the engineers at Somnia Incorporated, and he enjoyed his job. But he also enjoyed a quiet little nap after lunch every now and then. Sometimes after a nice soup-and-sandwich combo, he loved to creep into the toilet cubicle, rest his head against the wall and nod off for a few minutes before it was time to start work again.

That day Kevin had enjoyed a particularly large lunch. At 1.40 p.m., with twenty minutes to go before he had to clock on again, he felt an irresistible tiredness creeping over him. He bundled up his white coat to make a pillow, and was almost immediately happily dozing.

As Kevin was snoozing in the toilet, he had a dream. It started out as a lovely dream – he was at a riverside restaurant staffed entirely by badgers. They even danced and sang as they took your order – it was brilliant. In the toilet cubicle, Kevin's face broke into a smile as he ordered strawberry ice cream from the badger head waiter, and the other badgers all did a little coordinated dance routine as they went to fetch it for him. Then he became aware that somebody else had walked into the restaurant. He turned his head and his jaw dropped in

HORROR.

Lilith Delamere was standing in the doorway, her face like a thundercloud. The badgers took one look at her and dived for cover behind the bar with a terrified bleating.

'HOPPER!' she shrieked. 'What on earth do you think you're doing? Do you think I pay you to have a nice little nap?'

Kevin's brain reeled. Part of him knew he was asleep, and that he wasn't really about to be served ice cream by badgers. But that same part of his brain was also telling him that it was completely impossible for his boss to have walked into his dream and be telling him off. And, it added, he was on his lunch break anyway.

'Would you like to sit down and order something from the badgers, Ms Delamere?' he heard himself say. It's not easy to control what you say to people in dreams – they're tricksy things.

'No, I would not!' shrieked an outraged Lilith. 'Wake up and stop slacking off! Get back to work!' She turned on her heel and stalked out of the restaurant.

When Kevin woke up in the toilet cubicle a few minutes later and wiped the drool off his chin, the dream was vivid in his mind. But he shook his head and unrolled his white coat, preparing to head back to work. It just wasn't possible.

In the central laboratory, Lilith was smiling

delightedly as the dome was removed from her head. 'Congratulations, Professor,' she said. 'This is the breakthrough we've been looking for. You realize what your invention means, of course?'

'I think I do, Lilith,' replied a beaming Professor Dexter. 'I really think I do.'

They both then spoke at exactly the same time.

'We can discover so much more about the human imagination!' said the professor eagerly.

'We can banish bad dreams for ever!' said Lilith hungrily.

'Sorry, what?' they both said at the same time.

'I said, we can banish bad dreams for ever!' Lilith repeated. 'Why, what did you want to do?'

'Erm, discover much more about the human imagination?' said the professor, experiencing a horrible

sinking feeling that his vision wasn't shared by the person in charge. 'We can . . . help people share their dreams? Help them understand more about each other? And, erm . . .' He trailed off. Lilith Delamere was looking at him as if he were a slug who'd just suggested they have a nice day out at the salt museum.

'The human imagination?' she said, in a scandalized half-whisper, as if they were disgusting swear words. 'Share dreams? What on earth are you blathering about, man?'

You know that expression, 'feeling like the rug has been pulled from underneath you'? Well, Professor Dexter was feeling as if the rug had been pulled from underneath him, wrapped round about seventeen sturdy house bricks and then used to hit him firmly on the top of the head.

'BANISH BAD DREAMS FOR EVER . . .'

he thought to himself. Was that really what Lilith wanted to do with his invention?

Lilith was also feeling as if the rug had been pulled from underneath her feet. But she was a quick thinker. She realized two things almost immediately.

First, the professor had very different ideas about what his incredible technology could – and should – be used for.

But secondly, she still needed him to finish building his invention.

To continue the rug metaphor, she managed to keep her feet steady on the betuggened rug, like Aladdin wearing Velcro slippers. She forced her face into a strained, insincere smile.

'That is to say,' she fluted, 'the human imagination. Yes, absolutely. I was just a little taken aback for a moment.'

'The hypnagogic energy enhancement process can be a little discombobulating,' said the professor uncertainly. 'But you, er, said something about wanting to banish dreams?'

'Oh no, no, no.' Lilith waved an airy hand. 'I misspoke. I simply meant, we should aim to understand bad dreams better. Yes, understand. That's it.'

'Because we're not in the business of stealing dreams,' the professor cautioned. 'We're scientists, you know. Strictly observers.'

'Just as you say,' soothed Lilith. 'And for now, this discovery must be kept top, top secret. Tell nobody what you've discovered. Clear?'

'Absolutely crystal clear. Nobody will know.'

'Splendid,' Lilith replied, making a mental note to speak to General Pheare and make doubly sure this instruction was carried out.

*

'What on earth did you trust her for?' burst out Bin Bag, back in the castle courtyard of Professor Dexter's dream.

'I know, I know,' said the professor, looking sorrowful. 'I should have paid closer attention to the warning signs. But I was desperate to continue with my research. I thought that if I showed Lilith more about the Dream Field, she would come round to my way of thinking.'

'We've got a fix on the professor,' Maya heard Bea's voice say. 'Well done, Maya! Let me know when you're ready to come out!'

'Not yet!' said Maya desperately. 'Just a few more minutes. Dad, I need to know what happened. How did Lilith trick you?'

'Ah,' said the professor sadly. 'Yes, looking back now,

I should have **SEEN IT** coming . . .'

It's time for another flashback, but instead of singing a song we're just going to get straight on with it, in case that terrifying puffin comes back, OK?

Flashington flash, flashington flash.

Sorry.

SIX WEEKS AGO

'This is most impressive, Dexter. Most impressive.' Lilith gazed greedily at the control panel in the laboratory, now much more polished and high-tech than when she had first seen it. Professor Dexter was sitting in the chair in the centre of the lab, his eyes bright with excitement.

'I can't wait to show this to you, Lilith. It's really fascinating . . . and beautiful. Truly. I hope I'll be able to show you that nightmares are really nothing to be worried about.'

It was the early hours of the morning, and the Heptagon was largely deserted. But the central laboratory was brightly lit, the enormous space dwarfing the two figures who stood in the centre beside a single padded chair slung with circuit boards and wiring.

The professor continued, 'So, you're familiar with the controls?'

'Absolutely,' she trilled, examining the buttons in front of her. One was marked EXTRACT in large red letters. 'So this is the button I need to press to pull you back out of the dream, yes?'

'That's the most important button,' confirmed the professor. 'If you don't push that, my mind would remain in the Hypnagogic Field.'

'Trapped in a dream.' Lilith laughed. 'Well, we can't have that, can we? Don't worry, I'll pull you out whenever you tell me. After all, you might end up inside a nightmare.' Involuntarily, she shivered, remembering her own dreams from the two hours' sleep she'd managed to snatch the night before.

'Well, nightmares are fascinating in their own way,' argued the professor, sitting back in the chair and cracking his knuckles. 'I feel that they're caused by your brain trying to tell you something. I need a lot more research before I can be sure, of course, but I'm certain that bad dreams are to be explored, not ignored. Nothing unpleasant ever goes away just because you ignore it.'

'I'm sure you're right.' Lilith turned her back and smiled a smile nobody could see, a smile devoid of all warmth, as she reached out a long finger and touched a button marked ACTIVATE. With a whine, the metal dome descended and filled with pulsing golden light as the CHEESE device activated.

A large monitor in front of her showed a field of white static, but after a few moments vague shapes began to coalesce. Abruptly, Professor Dexter's voice rang out of the speakers on her control panel.

'WHOOAH!'

Lilith flicked a switch marked COMMUNICATE. 'Everything all right?'

'Just the Dream Drop,' he replied. 'Nearly there. Here we are.'

The picture on the screen cleared. Now Lilith could see the professor standing in a clear white space, surrounded by a circle of bright, shimmering images.

'As you can see,' he told her, 'I've managed to make everything much, much easier to see. I call this area the Zoetrope. Kind of a staging area for entering the Dream Field.'

'It's astonishing,' said Lilith honestly, peering at the screen. 'So, those pictures round the walls are . . .'

'Dreams. Exactly.'

'Dreams taking place . . . near here?'

'Not as near as the last time you saw this,' he replied. 'I've managed to extend the field a little. But none is more than half a mile away, I would guess. Ready to take a look?'

'Absolutely,' Lilith replied, her tired eyes gleaming with a strange, glazed light.

'The interface is simple,' the professor explained.

On the monitor Lilith saw him step forward and walk straight into the picture ahead of him. At once the scene changed. The clean white lines of the Zoetrope disappeared; he was now standing in a strange landscape of twisted, oddly shaped dark buildings.

'Ah, fascinating. We've certainly got ourselves a nightmare here,' came his voice out of the speakers. In the background Lilith could hear a high-pitched howling noise, and the hissing of a high wind. 'Whose head are we in here?' Professor Dexter asked her. 'Check the readout.'

Lilith examined a smaller screen next to the main monitor, marked DREAMER ID. 'This dream is being experienced by –' she read – 'someone called Lisa Trubble.'

'I think I can see her,' came Dexter's voice. 'Look.'

Lilith looked back at the main screen. The professor had ducked behind a low wall as a woman came running past. Her face wore an expression of terror and she threw a glance back over her shoulder before sprinting away.

'Yep, this is a nightmare all right,' he confirmed.

'A classic pursuit scenario.'

'It looks terrifying,' said Lilith softly, watching the screen.

'Instructional,' corrected the professor. 'Whatever Lisa is being chased by, it's something inside her own head. She's never going to be able to come to terms with it if she keeps running away. That's just one of the things I hope to be able to show people.'

But Lilith wasn't really listening. She was greedily running her eyes over the control panel. The professor's technology was complete. One of her other scientists would be able to adapt it for her own ends – someone easier to control than Professor Dexter. In fact, with his strange ideas about sharing dreams and understanding them, Clayton was now nothing more than a hindrance. Lilith knew she was going to have to keep him out of action until she had completed her plans. By the time she finally released him from his own nightmare, it would be too late: all dreams would be completely under her control.

'I'm heading back to the Zoetrope,' his voice came out of the speakers. 'I'll show you a couple more dreams before you extract me, if you like. Then I must be getting home – they'll be wondering where on earth I've got to!'

'Absolutely,' purred Lilith, moving over to the chair and looking down at the professor's sleeping form. Her lips twitched a little. Then, in one smooth movement, she pulled the metal dome away away from his head. There was a burst of static from the monitor, and a crackly voice.

'Hey! Is there a problem with the CHEESE? I'm losing the Zoetrope! Quickly! Extract me before it –'

WITH A FINAL FIZZ, ## HIS VOICE

VANISHED.

*

'So she took the dome away without extracting his mind from the dream?

That **HORRIBLE**,

SNIDEY,

NASTY,

SCHEMING OLD . . .

SNOTGOBBLER,'

Maya sputtered in fury a few minutes later. After a brief but emotional goodbye with her father, Bea had pulled Maya out of the dream. She was once again sitting in the NAP chair in the back of the van, shaking with rage.

'She'll get her just deserts, don't worry,' Bea soothed her, looking over sympathetically from her control desk.

'And not just desserts,' added Teddy. 'A cheese course, too. With crackers. Plus coffee and one of those little round mints. And a fortune cookie.'

'Yes, we get the picture, Teddy, thank you,' said Bea. 'You've done brilliantly, Maya! I've now got a firm fix on the professor's position in his dream. We can extract him using our own NAP chair and he can help us defeat Lilith and stop her plans!'

'Fantastic!' said Maya, leaping out of the chair expectantly. 'Let's do it!'

There was a moment of slightly embarrassed silence.

'Er, Maya,' said Bea gently. 'We can't use the NAP chair to pull him out of the Dream Field unless he's actually, you know . . . sitting in it?'

'Oh, right,' said Maya slowly. Then her eyes widened as realization dawned on her. 'You mean we've got to –'

'Break into the hospital and steal your unconscious dad?' Teddy replied. 'Yup, that's about the shape of it.'

'Sorry,' said Maya. 'Say that for me one more time, just so we're clear. We've got to break into *where now* and steal *what now*?'

CHAPTER 7
PHEARE AND FLAMEWOOD

Maya's mum had to spend almost five minutes trying to shake her awake the next morning. 'Come on! You're going to be late for school!' Maya groaned and tried to hide her head inside a folded pillow. It had been after four o'clock in the morning when she'd crept back in after her adventure with the Dream Bandits, and she'd been asleep for less than three hours.

'Sorry, Mum,' she mumbled, forcing herself to sit up. 'Didn't sleep too well last night. I was having this . . .' She tailed off when she saw Bin Bag sitting at the end of the bed staring at her. '. . . this really, really vivid dream,' she finished in a whisper, as the events of last night crowded back into her brain.

'Well, breakfast's ready,' her mum told her, ruffling her hair affectionately. 'I'm pretty tired myself – I was up until late working on some blueprints for that new sports centre. I'm taking them into the office this morning. If you're quick, I can drop you at school on the way.'

Chewing toast, Maya pondered the events of the night before. Oddly, the dream with the talking cat and the waking professor seemed more real and exciting than this rather boring Thursday morning where the cat simply miaowed and her father was still in hospital, asleep. She kept drifting back into the dream inside her head, seeing her father sitting calmly in the castle courtyard, and had to snap herself to attention to avoid falling forward into the marmalade.

'You really are sleepy, aren't you?' said her mum, feeling her forehead in concern. 'I can pick you up after school as well, if you like.'

Maya was desperately tempted to tell her everything and ask for help. But something Teddy had said just before he'd dropped her at home kept coming back to her. 'These people are mean, and they stop at nothing,' he had warned her. 'They've already taken your dad out of action. Anyone who knows about it becomes a target.

SO DON'T. TELL. ANYONE.'

'Actually, I'm meeting some friends after school,' she told her mum, who started back in mock surprise.

'Oh, that's wonderful! You haven't been hanging around with friends for weeks. Just keep your phone on you, OK?' Her mum spun the car keys round a finger. 'Ready?'

After school, Maya took a serpentine route to the Flamewoods' address. 'Make sure you're not followed,' Teddy had told her seriously. 'Double back on yourself, and keep changing hats if possible.'

'Don't be ridiculous, Teddy,' Bea had told him. 'Maya doesn't have an unlimited supply of different hats. Just go round the streets a bit – check that Lilith's goons aren't tailing you.'

After circling the same block several times, peering over her shoulder at intervals, Maya felt it was safe to head to the mattress showroom.

As instructed, she went round the back and was relieved to see Bea waving from an upstairs window. 'Hang on,' she called, 'I'll come and let you in the back way. If you go in through the shop, Dad's bound to try and sell you a new mattress.'

A few minutes later, Maya was holding a cup of tea and sitting opposite Teddy and Bea in their large, cluttered apartment above the showroom. 'OK,' she told them, 'I'm in. Let's rob a hospital.'

'Yes!' Teddy punched the air delightedly. 'I've always wanted an actual heist to organize. This is going to be amazing!'

'There's just one question I want you to answer first,' said Maya, holding up a cautionary finger. 'Why are you trying to rescue my dad? What's in this for you?'

You might be surprised that Maya hadn't asked this sooner, but give her a break. She's having a difficult week.

'Ah, good question.' Bea looked slightly embarrassed. 'Well, the thing is . . .'

'Basically, our mum's one of the bad guys,' Teddy finished for her.

'Teddy!' exclaimed Bea. 'She's not bad! She's just, you know . . .'

'Compromised!' said Teddy, delighted to get a real-life opportunity to use the kind of dialogue his favourite spy films were full of. 'She's been turned by the enemy! She's a double agent, only she's not. She's a single agent! Only on the wrong side. You know, one of the baddies,' he finished rather lamely.

'Let me get this straight,' said Maya, holding up a hand in the universally recognized signal for 'shush'. 'Your mum is working for Lilith?'

'Only because they're forcing her to!' protested Bea. 'We heard the whole thing – and that's when we decided we had to help!'

'You heard? How?' Maya demanded.

'Well, it was like this . . .' began Teddy.

And Teddy and Bea told Maya what had happened at the mattress showroom five weeks earlier.

WHAT'S THAT?

Oh, you want to know what happened as well? At the mattress showroom five weeks earlier? You'd like us to tell you by means of another flashback?

OK – you bought the book, so we guess you're the boss. Here you go. Best flashbacking trousers on, everybody, it's time to find out what happened . . .

FIVE WEEKS EARLIER . . .

(Make a harp sound effect with your mouth here to denote the rewinding of time.)

FIVE WEEKS AGO

'This is the place, sir.' General Pheare held open the door of Matt's Mattresses and Lilith Delamere strode past him as if she owned the place. She didn't – she already owned a successful sleep-science laboratory and wasn't looking to extend her brand, even though a mattress showroom would have been what a business person would call a complementary acquisition for her portfolio.

Anyway, Lilith looked out across the rows and rows of beds, narrowing her eyes into their meanest, most intimidating expression. The expression was completely lost on the man who was now weaving his way towards her through the warehouse, waving cheerily.

'Good morning, good morning, and welcome to Matt's Mattresses!' he called. 'You, madam, I can already tell, are a lady who appreciates a bit of comfort. And you have very much come to the right place. This is the one and only home of Flamewood Floaty Foam!'

'I'm not here to buy a mattress, you ridiculous little man,' Lilith sneered. 'I am here to speak to your wife. Where is she?'

'Oh, the queen bee?' chirped Matt Flamewood. 'The boss? The head teacher? The, er, first lady?'

'If you mean your wife, Julia Flamewood,' said Lilith, cutting into this annoying list, 'then, yes. I need to speak to her.' Her expression had grown so chilly it was now cold enough to function as an efficient air-conditioning system for a medium-sized office block. But, sadly, not cold enough to dampen Matt Flamewood's roguish banter.

'Just skip up the old spindly staircase,' he said, pointing to a large set of metal stairs that climbed the wall at the back of the showroom. 'Throw a Lucy-left at the top, then it's the second door on the Ruby-right.' He was a master salesman, and the first rule of being a master salesman was: never be discouraged. Not even when the customer looks like she wants to tear you into pieces and stamp on each piece separately while screaming the words, 'I Hate You.' Which is exactly how Lilith was looking at that precise moment. Without a word, she turned on her heel and marched towards the staircase.

'Oooh, someone got out of the wrong side of bed this

morning,' said Matt to General Pheare, who was still dithering by the door. 'Or rather, someone slept on the wrong mattress last night! Did you know that scientific studies show that a great night's sleep can increase your good mood by a factor of as much as seven thousand per cent?'

'What?' replied Pheare, briefly baffled by this statistic. 'That's ridiculous!'

'I'll tell you what's ridiculous,' Mr Flamewood continued, walking over to Pheare, putting an arm round his shoulders and propelling him across the showroom at a near-run. Pheare stumbled slightly in his oversized boots but the firm arm held him upright. 'It's ridiculous to sleep on something that's not as comfortable as this!' Mr Flamewood had led him to a huge bed, covered with a satiny bedspread and sprinkled with puffy cushions. 'The super-size emperor deluxe! Have a go!' And, with that, he pushed Pheare backwards on to the bed, where he rolled around like an upended turtle.

'**HOO HOO!** That's right, have a good old bounce around!' the salesman encouraged him.

Pheare's legs flailed as he tried to force himself upright. But he couldn't get a purchase on the bouncy surface, and kept rolling towards the centre of the bed like a ball settling into the centre of a roulette wheel.

'Comfy, isn't it?' declared Matt Flamewood delightedly. 'It's like you never want to get out of bed! Although, for a heavier gentleman such as yourself, I might be tempted to recommend a slightly firmer –'

'**SILENCE!**' Pheare squealed, his voice cracking embarrassingly as, with one final flail, he managed to propel himself over the opposite edge of the bed, where he landed on the floor with a dull **THUD**.

*

The Flamewoods lived in a huge, open-plan apartment above the mattress showroom. It stretched the entire length of the building, with massive high windows that reached all the way up to its beamed ceiling. That might not mean much to a lot of our readers, but we know that many estate agents enjoy reading to their children, and those architectural details are just for them.

The bedrooms were at either end of the apartment, and in between was an enormous living area, cluttered with tables and squashy sofas. Old rugs were strewn across the wooden floor. (This paragraph is for any interior designers who might also be reading – we don't want them to feel left out.)

At one of the large wooden tables, Doctor Julia Flamewood was sitting in a patch of sunlight that streamed through the windows, tapping at a laptop. She raised her head as the apartment filled with a hideous **clanging**, as if someone were ringing an extremely badly made bell right beside her left ear. Someone was coming up the metal staircase from the showroom – and that someone was walking much, much too loudly. They were stamping as if they were really, really cross with the floor.

Julia furrowed her brow. Her husband didn't normally come upstairs during the day – he was always busy smashing his own self-imposed mattress sales targets. And the twins were busy as usual, messing around in the showroom or the large warehouse area at the back of it. They often spent hours playing hide-and-seek among the rows and rows of bed frames and mattresses. So who could possibly be marching up to her home at this time of day?

Her question was answered a few seconds later when the door was flung open, revealing a tall, slim silhouette.

'Lilith!' Julia gasped, startled to see her boss from Somnia Incorporated suddenly appear at her home. As one of Professor Dexter's team of engineers, Julia had been involved with his development of the

CHEESE system, but she didn't have much contact with Lilith.

'Doctor Flamewood,' Lilith purred as she stepped over the threshold. 'May I come in?' She walked across the room and sat down.

'You appear to have already come in,' replied Julia smoothly, trying to keep calm. What on earth was the company's chief executive doing at her house? Her mind ranged back over the last few weeks, wondering what she could possibly have done wrong. Guiltily, she realized that she'd snaffled a box of paperclips a few days ago – a box of paperclips that was, even now, sitting on the table between them.

'So, what seems to be the problem?' she asked nervously. 'If it's about the paperclips, I was going to bring them back. I just needed –'

'Paperclips?' Lilith sneered. 'Oh no, Julia. This is much, much bigger than paperclips.'

'Well, to be fair, most things are,' said Julia, trying to lighten the mood – and failing.

'I am here,' Lilith went on, 'because I need your help with something.'

There was a pause. Julia's natural politeness was urging her to offer her boss a cup of tea, but she resisted. There was something so cold and arrogant about the way Lilith had marched into her home that Julia felt she'd be unable to drink out of any mug Lilith had used. And Julia really liked all of her mugs.

'You're aware, of course, of the unfortunate accident that befell your colleague Professor Dexter recently,' said Lilith smoothly.

It almost looked as if Lilith's thin mouth puckered into a slight smile as she said this. Julia frowned. 'Yes, it was awful,' she said carefully. 'An awful, awful accident.'

'Accident?' mused Lilith. 'An accident, was it? Was it really?'

'Well, you just called it an accident,' Julia replied, but Lilith was holding up a finger for silence.

'What if it wasn't an accident?' she said in a quiet, cold voice. 'What if it was . . . a punishment? Something that happens to people who don't follow orders?' She leaned forward and tapped the table sharply three times to emphasize these last three words.

'**WHAT?**' sputtered Julia, suddenly terrified. She couldn't believe she was hearing this.

'I'm sure you wouldn't want any similar . . . accident to happen to a member of your own family, now, would you?' said Lilith in a tone of mock concern.

'My . . . f-family?' stuttered Julia. 'I'd do anything to protect them. Anything!'

'Anything?' Lilith leaned back in her chair and raised her eyebrows. 'Excellent, Julia. That's really excellent. You'd do anything to protect your family. Hold that thought –' she leaned forward again – 'and listen to me very, very carefully . . .'

A few minutes later, Matt Flamewood looked up from his desk, where he was filling in some forms about the brand-new mattress he'd just sold. 'Find the missus all right, did you?' he called cheerily to Lilith as she stalked back down the stairs. She waved a dismissive hand in reply, before noticing General Pheare sitting at the table opposite Matt.

'Pheare!' she barked. 'What do you think you're doing?'

'He's preparing to enjoy the best forty winks of his

life, that's what he's doing!' crowed Matt Flamewood. 'He's about to snuggle down on a brand-new, state-of-the-art Flamewood Five Fifty, featuring Flamewood Floaty Foam!'

'Come with me,' snapped Lilith. Pheare scribbled a quick signature and scrambled to his feet, stumbling slightly as his size-ten boot came away from his size-seven heel.

'Coming, sir,' he puffed. 'If you could just give me a hand carrying my new mattress to the car?'

Upstairs, Julia Flamewood heard Lilith's shouts of rage echoing faintly through the showroom, but she had more important things to worry about. She pressed an anxious knuckle to her mouth, remembering the instructions she'd just been given. *Tell nobody what you're doing*, Lilith had told her. *Not your husband, not your children. Because if you do, we'll find out. And if we find out – they'll meet with an accident, just like your friend Professor Dexter.*

I've got no choice, she thought to herself desperately. *I'm going to have to do whatever she wants.*

Lilith pushed through the doors of Matt's Mattresses and strode away, leaving General Pheare to struggle home with his new mattress. She was feeling really rather smug. Julia Flamewood would help with the secret project, she thought to herself, and – crucially – she would never dare tell anyone. The whole plan would be kept completely secret. Sadly for Lilith, but pleasingly for the rest of us, she was completely and utterly wrong.

Because what she didn't realize was that her entire conversation had been overheard. Squeezed into a small wooden cupboard underneath the Flamewoods' TV was a pair of ears. Not just a pair of ears, obviously – that would be weird. They were Teddy's ears – and they were attached to the rest of Teddy. He had managed to find an excellent hiding place, squashing his knees right up on either side of his head to stuff himself into the cupboard. Bea would never find him this time, he

thought to himself as he carefully closed the door. A little while later he was thinking to himself, *Who's that coming in to talk to Mum?* Then a minute or so after that he was thinking, *This is amazing. I'm actually overhearing a real-life plot, like an actual spy.* By the time his mother had left the room, he was mainly thinking this: *I can no longer feel my legs.* But also this: *I've got to tell Bea what's happened so we can make a plan to save Mum! Just as soon as I can walk again.*

*

'WHAT?'

said Bea incredulously ten minutes later. Teddy, after an energetic dozen star jumps to get his legs working again, had dragged his sister into the warehouse. They were right at the back, next to a row of parked electric vans and a pile of cardboard boxes full of posters showing their dad's grinning face and the slogan, MATT FLAMEWOOD GUARANTEES YOU A BOUNCY BEDTIME! 'He's got to re-write that,' muttered Bea under her breath, catching sight of one of them.

'I was like a real-life secret agent, Bea!' explained Flamewood – Teddy Flamewood – excitedly. 'Neither of them had any idea I was there! I was like a cupboard ninja! Totally silent!'

'Yes, yes, very impressive,' said Bea impatiently. 'But I was actually asking – what did she say they did to Professor Dexter?'

'She said they, you know, knocked him out somehow! Permanently!' Teddy replied excitedly. 'It's a classic bad-guy move – if someone finds out your plot, you take them out of the picture! It's dastardly, as they'd say in the old days. And now they're forcing Mum to help them!'

'This is serious.' Bea gnawed anxiously on a thumbnail. 'We're going to have to help her – but we can't tell anyone. If Lilith finds out anyone else knows –'

'One of us will meet with an accident, just like the prof,' agreed Teddy seriously.

'Right,' said Bea. 'Let's think about this. The most important thing –'

'Is what we call ourselves? You're right!' Teddy broke in. 'I was thinking – Super Spy Teddy Flamewood and his faithful sidekick, Science Girl.'

'For a start,' said Bea, 'I'm not your sidekick. If anything, you're mine. And the name "Science Girl" is patronizing. But there's no time for that now. I was about to say, the most important thing is – we need to find out what Lilith's planning. What evil, secret scheme is she forcing Mum to help her with?'

'Right!' Teddy agreed. 'So, we need to kidnap her, get some of that really strong sticky tape and a chair –'

'No, no, NO!'

Bea scolded. 'How many times, Teddy? This is real life, not one of those stupid films. Listen. There's only one person who can tell us what Lilith's planning, and how she can be stopped.'

'James Bond!'

'No!' Bea exclaimed patiently. 'Not James Bond. James Bond is a fictional character.'

'Jason Bourne, then.'

'Again . . . Look, never mind. No – I'm talking about Professor Dexter.' Bea took a step back in satisfaction as her brother stared at her, dumbfounded.

'Professor Dexter? Have you gone mad?' blurted Teddy. 'I saw him when Mum took me to work with her once; he was wearing some mad scarf and muttering to himself. Hardly secret-agent material!'

'We're not looking for a secret agent, genius,' Bea corrected him. 'We're looking for an expert who can help us figure out what Lilith's planning. Professor Dexter's the head of the research team that Mum works on, remember? He's the brains behind all the stuff she's been raving about, the dream thingy.'

'Yes, but . . .' Teddy was regarding her pityingly. 'In case you hadn't noticed, the prof is fast asleep. There's no way of talking to someone who's fast asleep.'

'That,' Bea told him, smiling broadly, 'is where you are – as usual – completely and utterly wrong.'

If this were a film, there would be a montage at this point. If you don't know what a montage is, it's when there's a series of brief scenes to indicate something exciting is happening quite gradually, but it would be boring to watch it unfold, so here are the highlights. Kind of hard to pull off in a book, but we'll give it a try.

To begin the montage, please put on some pumping rock music and then spend a couple of minutes playing out each of these mini scenes in your head.

* Bea hacks into her mum's laptop as Teddy excitedly watches over her shoulder. They find a folder entitled

TOP SECRET: DREAM PROJECT.

Bea opens up the folder and the screen fills with complicated diagrams.

* Bea sits at a workbench with a soldering iron, bending over a smoking circuit board. Teddy is playing air guitar with a broom in the background. Bea leans over and consults a large notebook on the bench beside her. On the cover is written in large letters:

BEA'S TOP-SECRET DREAM LOGBOOK
Do not read on pain of being in extreme pain.

* 'Dad, this van needs a service,' Bea tells her father. 'I'm going to take it into the workshop for a couple of weeks, OK?' Matt Flamewood smiles and nods cheerily but we cut away from this scene before he can do anything more embarrassing.

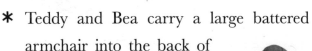

* Teddy and Bea carry a large battered armchair into the back of the van.

* Bea looks up from her workbench as Teddy struggles in with a plastic dome in his arms. 'Look what I found in a skip out the back of Krazy Kutts!' he tells her. 'It'll be perfect for our Dream Dome once I give it a bit of a wash.'

* Bea connects complicated wiring to the chair, which is now fixed in the back of the van, with the dome hinged on to the headrest. In the background, Teddy is hanging a pair of furry dice from the rear-view mirror.

* Bea throws a switch and the control panels in the back of the van flicker into life. She punches the air in satisfaction. In the background, Teddy is eating a doughnut with pink frosting. Suddenly he spits out a mouthful of doughnut, eyes widening in excitement. He's had an idea.

'Dream Bandits!' he yells excitedly. 'That's what we'll call ourselves! The Dream Bandits! Now let's go and rescue that professor!'

The pumping rock music is carefully edited to end at this exact moment.

End of montage! Wasn't that fun? And it advanced the plot without taking up too much of your valuable time.

*

Back in the present day (you can mark this with an extra harp noise if you like, but it's optional), Maya took a sip of her tea and discovered that it had gone stone cold while Teddy and Bea had been telling their story. 'So, is this your dream notebook?' she asked, reaching across the table. Bea nodded, pointing to the words on the cover: BEA'S TOP-SECRET DREAM LOGBOOK, DO NOT READ ON PAIN OF BEING IN EXTREME PAIN.

Maya flicked the cover open and gasped out loud. In large letters on the very first page were the words,

'Where did you hear that?' she demanded. 'That's what's written on the wall of my dad's workshop!'

'It's also what's written all over the documents we found on Mum's computer, telling us how to create the NAP chair,' Bea countered.

'Yeah,' confirmed Teddy, 'most of the pages have it written at the top. It's kind of become the Dream Bandits' motto.'

Maya pondered this for a moment. It was just like her dad to write WHAT IF?, across a scientific document. She felt a rush of pride that his ideas had trickled down through his team of researchers to the two new friends sitting opposite her. 'It's my dad's motto as well,' she said, smiling. 'But I don't think he'll mind sharing it.'

Turning back to the notebook, she flicked over a few more pages at random. There were several drawings of the NAP chair and the oval CHEESE device that made it work, all annotated in Bea's small, neat handwriting. '*Successful test number one!*' she read out loud. '*Teddy was able to enter a live dream tonight for the first time, although he squealed like a frightened shrew when he experienced the Dream Drop.*'

'Oi!' Teddy complained.

'*We have located the dream where Professor Dexter must be imprisoned,*' Maya read on another page. '*But after two hours Teddy was still unable to locate him. What are we missing?*' The next page began with the words WHAT IF? once again as a title.

'That's what we write whenever we get stuck,' explained Bea, standing up and coming to read over

Maya's shoulder. 'It usually helps.'

'*What if it's the wrong dream?*' read Maya aloud. '*What if he's hiding in there? What if there's some reason we're not able to find him? What if we need to send someone else to look for him? What if there's someone who might do a better job of locating the professor? What if someone knows something about him that might help?*' And then, underlined several times at the bottom of the page, were the words,

in large letters.

'And that's where I come in?' asked Maya, grinning. After so many weeks of feeling completely alone, the sensation of being part of a team was like stepping out of a cold, dark cave into blazing hot sunshine. She was filled with sudden hope – so powerful it made her fingers tingle.

'And that's where you come in!' confirmed Teddy and Bea in unison.

'We thought if anyone could find him, it would be you. But we had to do it secretly,' said Teddy. 'So I sneaked into your dream and recruited you!'

'Welcome to the Dream Bandits,' added Bea, making Maya feel even more sunshiny. 'Now, who wants a fresh cup of tea? We've got a hospital heist to plan.'

CHAPTER 8
THE DREAM MACHINE

'Welcome, ladies and gentlemen. Welcome to the future.'

Lilith Delamere looked out across the crescent of expectant faces ranged in front of her: the faces of two dozen smartly dressed and extremely rich-looking people. The bright lights of the Heptagon's huge, seven-sided central laboratory were reflected in over-polished shoes and teeth, and forty-eight eyes that were all shining with greed.

The audience that Lilith had gathered for her demonstration consisted of representatives of the world's richest companies. And they had all been lured here with the promise of a discovery that would make them an enormous amount of money. They craned their necks to look over Lilith's shoulder at what might be in store for them, and how it could make them even richer than they already were. At first glance there was nothing much to see, simply seven tidily made beds arranged round a huge bank of machinery in the centre of the lab. There was a complicated-looking control desk with no one sitting in its single chair, and the beds, too, were empty. Above each bed hung a large, flat, blank screen.

'I'm sure you're all very anxious to see what we've been working on,' Lilith told the audience, 'so I won't keep you waiting long. What I have to offer you today is, quite simply, the most breathtaking scientific discovery the human race has ever made.' There were one or two nervous chuckles at this – surely this tall, dark-haired

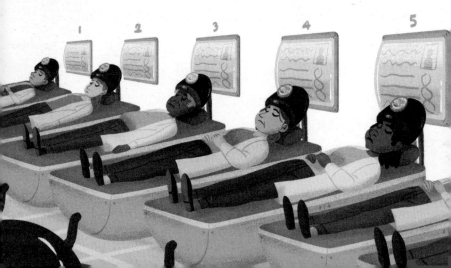

woman with enormous bags under her eyes was joking? 'I can assure you, this is no joke,' she went on stridently. The chuckles died away. 'But perhaps it's best if you see my invention for yourselves. I'm confident that, once you do, you won't feel like laughing at me.' A couple of faces reddened at this.

Lilith clicked her fingers and a door in one of the laboratory's seven sides slid smoothly sideways. Try reading that sentence aloud five times in a row. Out marched Doctor Julia Flamewood, stony-faced, leading seven white-coated scientists. They marched into the room in neat single file, each scientist proceeding to one of the beds and lying down. Julia herself took up position at the control desk and began clacking professionally at a computer keyboard.

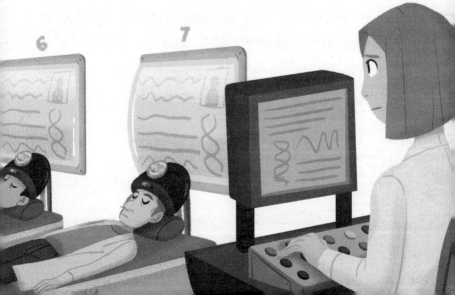

'For countless centuries,' Lilith told her congregation of business people, 'humankind has dealt with the dangers it has faced. From our earliest days as cave-people we have confronted the things we find frightening, and conquered them. But there is one part of our lives we have been unable to control. Our dreams.' She clicked her fingers again, and Julia, with only a slight hesitation, flicked a row of switches downwards. The huge column of machinery in the middle of the beds began to emit a loud, deep humming, and coloured lights began to flash. Each of the seven screens flickered into life, though at the moment they were only showing fizzing black-and-white static.

'Since the dawn of time,' Lilith was now saying, 'we have been terrorized by nightmares. Terrors that haunt us while we sleep. Dreams of being chased, or humiliated and laughed at.' Her voice caught slightly at the end of this sentence, and – though nobody noticed – her eyes flickered upward towards the office where the portrait of her father hung. But she quickly collected herself. 'No more,' she almost shouted, gripping the sides of her lectern until her knuckles turned white.

'I have eliminated nightmares for ever! I have freed us from the tyranny of our own sleeping minds. Ladies and gentlemen, I give you a device I have named . . .

THE CLEAN SLEEP!'

At the third and final click of Lilith's long fingers, Doctor Julia Flamewood pulled a large lever in the centre of the control console. Thin beams of a garish green light shot out of the machine straight into the heads of the seven scientists in the beds. The audience saw them immediately fall asleep, arms and heads flopping as if they'd been knocked out. And at the same time, each screen above each bed began showing an image. The one directly behind Lilith now bore a picture of lapping waves on a beach. The ones on either side showed a tranquil river bank and a small copse of trees, their leaves fluttering in a light breeze.

Julia Flamewood looked up at the column of machinery in dismay. Since Lilith had threatened her, she had been helping Lilith recreate Professor Dexter's dream technology to complete this machine. When she had been told exactly what it was for, she had been aghast, but Lilith had once again explained to her in no uncertain terms that if she didn't do exactly as she was told, she or her family would be imprisoned inside a dream. Thinking helplessly of her husband and children, she'd had no choice but to comply.

'On the screens,' Lilith said, speaking now in a more hushed tone, 'you can see the dreams that are being beamed directly into my test subjects' brains. Lovely, calming images. No danger of any kind of nightmare. Just these beautiful, restful dreams all night long. Please, have a walk around and see for yourselves.' There was a scraping of chair legs as the audience members got to their feet and began to wander curiously round the laboratory. The sleeping scientist on the other side of the Clean Sleep was apparently dreaming of a crackling log fire. The man next to her was seeing a playful kitten with a ball of wool. But after a while the same question began to occur to a lot of the rich, successful people in the room. The same question that rich, successful people spend a lot of time asking in almost any situation. And finally one of them said it out loud.

'So how are we supposed to make money out of this?' demanded a plump, florid-faced man in a dark blue suit that artfully didn't quite conceal his eye-wateringly expensive watch. 'I mean, I'm sure it's very *clever* . . .' His tone of voice made it clear that he didn't think being clever was particularly impressive. 'But where's the profit potential? The monetization? Is it scalable?' Heads began to nod around the room. *We* might not be familiar with some of that vocabulary but *they* all spoke the language of greed fluently.

'I'm so glad you asked,' purred Lilith, walking over to him and patting him patronizingly on a beefy shoulder. 'Mr . . .?'

'The name's Philpott,' he told her. 'Philpott's Cereals.'

'Ah, yes, of course,' cooed Lilith. Philpott's was the largest manufacturer of breakfast cereals on the planet. (Clearly Philpott's isn't a real thing; we've made it up for legal reasons. We're not allowed to use the name of the real cereal people in case they kick off about it. So, for the purposes of this story, just imagine that everyone loves tucking into Philpott's Phrosty Phlakes every morning, OK? Sorry for that glimpse behind the curtain, but we feel it's important to be honest with our readers. Onward, there's another good bit coming up.)

Lilith called out to Julia Flamewood at the control desk, 'Insert the Philpott's advertisement into Dream Station Five, please.' Again with that tiny hesitation, Julia tapped at her keyboard. Grabbing Mr Philpott by the arm, Lilith led him across to one of the beds and silently pointed at the screen above it. The sleeping scientist here was apparently dreaming an extremely dull dream about a babbling brook. But suddenly a man walked into shot and sat down beside the stream, eating a bowl of cereal. 'Yum,' said the man, looking directly at the camera, 'these Phrosty Phlakes really are delicious! There's nothing you want to eat when you wake up except a nourishing, tasty bowl of Phrosty Phlakes. They'rrrrrrrre . . . good!' (For legal reasons, this is different to any other slogan associated with any other cereals.) With a wink, the man walked out of shot.

'Wake up Station Five,' Lilith instructed

Julia, who reached over and flicked a switch. The ray of light above the scientist went out, and she sat up in bed looking groggy.

'How do you feel?' asked Mr Philpott eagerly.

'Terrible –' the scientist started to say, but Lilith interrupted.

'Never mind that,' she snapped. 'What do you want for *breakfast*?'

The scientist furrowed her brow. 'This is weird,' she said, yawning, 'but I've got this terrible craving for a bowl of that sugary stuff the kids always want . . . What's it called . . .?'

'Philpott's Phrosty Phlakes?' asked Mr Philpott eagerly, his eyes shining.

'Yes, that's them,' said the baffled-looking scientist. 'It's weird. I've never liked them . . . I normally just have a cup of –'

'Thank you, thank you,' Lilith broke in. 'We don't need to hear your entire brunch menu.' She gave an unconvincing, tinkling little laugh. 'But I think we can agree, Mr Philpott,' she went on, drawing him away, 'that your company has just gained a new loyal customer. And what about you?' She turned to another woman among the crowd. 'You represent a car company, I believe?'

'That's right,' said the woman. 'Road Runner.' (Again this bears no relation to any real car company with or without the same initials.)

'Nice cars,' said Lilith, a little dismissively. 'But with my help, they could quite easily become . . . the car of your dreams!' She gestured to Julia, and suddenly on the screen nearest to them, a shiny new SUV pulled into shot. 'The all-new Road Runner Deluxe,' said a deep, authoritative voice. 'It's the only car for you. Your current car is not as good as a Road Runner. You should change it immediately, otherwise your friends will all think you're a failure.'

'I just have this overpowering need to get a new car,' said the scientist on Dream Station Six a few moments later when Lilith had him woken up. 'I just realized that my car's not good enough. I've got to buy one of those Road Runners.'

'This is extraordinary,' said another of the assembled business people.

'She can quite literally put advertisements in people's dreams,' marvelled another.

'Ladies and gentlemen, ladies and gentlemen,' said Lilith, holding up a hand to quell the hubbub. 'I told you this was the future, and I hope you can now see what I mean. Commercials that cannot be skipped past, or blocked, or ignored. I am offering the only way to get your corporate messaging directly into your clients' thoughts.'

'**HOW MUCH do you want for it?'**

shouted one of the audience. 'I'll double whatever anyone else is prepared to pay.'

'**I'll TREBLE it!'**

shouted another. 'I'll pay whatever it takes to get my hands on this!'

'**I'll QUAD … QUINT … I'll pay MORE!'**

another yelled, jostling towards the front of the crowd.

Lilith Delamere smiled to herself. The demonstration had gone better than she could possibly have dreamed, ironically. Not that she personally liked dreaming, of course. But she was now sure that she'd have all the funding she needed to put her grand plan into action. 'No more nightmares,' she said to herself quietly, glancing upward once more towards her office and the portrait of Doctor Damian Delamere. 'No more nightmares for me . . . or for anybody. I will rescue us all.'

'Can somebody **PLEASE** get me a bowl of Phrosty Phlakes?'

yelled the scientist from Station Five, sounding more than a little unhinged.

CHAPTER 9
APOCALYPSE COW

'There he goes!' exclaimed Teddy Flamewood. 'Right on cue!'

'Yes, six p.m.,' confirmed Bea, tapping on her laptop. 'Somnia's head of security completes his daily inspection and leaves the hospital.'

The mattress van was parked up opposite Hagstone Court, concealed round a corner to avoid the prying eyes of the security cameras on either side of the gates. Teddy – absolutely in his element – was crouched forward in the passenger seat, eyes glued to a large pair of black binoculars that were propped up on the dashboard. Bea and Maya were staying out of sight in the back, Bea surrounded by wires and control panels, barely visible behind the NAP chair, which was powered down and empty. It was now two weeks since Maya had joined the Dream Bandits and planning for the big heist was well underway.

Maya had been flicking through the Dream Logbook, which she had now read so many times she practically knew it off by heart. Bea had detailed every part of their search for Professor Dexter, and asked constant questions about the dream technology that Maya found fascinating. *Tonight I managed to use the* CHEESE *to transmit a disguise to Teddy within the Zoetrope,* Bea had written beneath a picture of Teddy wearing a pirate's hat. *Could be useful on future dream missions.*

'Right. Let's see where his lair is, shall we?' offered Teddy, abandoning the binoculars and shuffling over to the driver's seat. He turned on the ignition and the van chugged out into the traffic, trailing the portly, beachball-esque form of Pheare as he weaved through the crowds of people heading home from work.

'It's not the most inconspicuous vehicle for secretly shadowing someone, is it?' mused Teddy. When they turned a corner, the giant mattress atop the van creaked as it rocked to and fro on its springs.

'You're the one who's always going on about hiding in plain sight,' Maya countered. She had begun to grow very fond of the van, with its dark, cluttered interior. After all, it was the vehicle that had brought her dad back to her. In a dream, at least.

For the past week, every day after school, Maya, Teddy and Bea had been staking out the hospital where, she now realized, her father was a prisoner rather than a patient. They had to plan this down to the last detail if they were to succeed. Maya's mum was delighted she was out seeing friends a lot more, which gave Maya an occasional pang of guilt. But, she told herself, this was all about rescuing her dad. And if her mum found out about their plans, it could put her in danger from General Pheare and his security operatives. Maya frowned at his broad, round back as they tailed him through the teatime traffic.

Some time later, Bea carefully updated her files after watching Pheare unlock the door of a house and head inside. 'That's it,' she said in a satisfied tone of voice. 'That's the head of security. We already know where the receptionist lives – and the guards who might have the code for that keypad Maya mentioned. We're ready.'

'Excellent,' said Teddy with a smile.

'TIME TO COMMENCE OPERATION HOSPITAL DREAM HEIST!'

'Terrible name,' complained Bea.

'Does what it says on the tin,' corrected Teddy. 'I never understood the point of calling things, like, Operation Sneaky Sea Lion, then having to explain what it actually is all the time.'

'Yes, yes, OK,' said Bea, sighing. She had heard this argument several times already.

'Time to activate our secret weapon, I think!' added Teddy. 'Operation Maya Hospital Dream Heist!'

'She's not exactly a secret weapon if her name's in the title of the operation, is she?' reasoned Bea, reasonably.

Teddy simply shrugged, which he correctly judged to be the most infuriating response possible to his sister's question.

*

Planning for the hospital heist had been taking place in Teddy and Bea's apartment above the mattress showroom. Teddy had watched enough films to know exactly how things should be done.

'Rule one of planning a secret mission like this one,' he told Maya and Bea, whipping a sheet away from a table to reveal a shoebox upon which he had written the word HOSPITAL, 'is that you must have a detailed scale model of the target, made of cardboard.'

'A *detailed* scale model?' queried Maya, who had already sketched a wonderful map of Hagstone Court for her fellow Dream Bandits. She was a little stung that, as the artist in the group, she hadn't been put on model duty.

'Well, OK,' Teddy conceded. 'I didn't have time to make it very detailed. But you can totally see what it's supposed to be, right?'

'Well, only because you've actually written the word HOSPITAL on it,' Maya complained.

'Rule two,' Teddy persisted, 'is that the heisters –'

'Heisters?' Bea broke in.

'Heisters,' Teddy insisted. 'Or heistketeers, if you prefer –'

'I don't.' Bea sniffed.

'Must travel to the target location in a battered old van,' finished Teddy, waving a hand towards the mattress van, which was parked just inside a large set of garage doors at the back of the warehouse. 'And rule three, in every gang of heistketeers there must be a nerdy one who stays in the van and does nerdy things on a laptop, like a huge nerd.'

'Cheers,' said Bea sarcastically.

'Pleasure.' Teddy gave a small bow and Maya couldn't stop herself breaking into a smile. Teddy was infuriating, sure, but there was something reassuring about his cocksure confidence. She was starting to believe they actually might be able to rescue her dad, and the thought made her feel like she'd been wrapped in a warm duvet after a cold swim.

'I hope you're taking this seriously, Teddy,' warned Bea, helping herself to a biscuit from a plate beside the cardboard box. Sorry, the scale model of the hospital.

'Course I am, sis!' Teddy protested. 'But rule four of secret-mission planning, as you well know, is that there needs to be a cool wisecracking one who's kind of irritating but gets the job done and walks off in slow motion at the end.'

'Which one am I, then?' asked Maya, also grabbing a biscuit.

'You're the green, wide-eyed newcomer who knows absolutely nothing but is keen to learn,' explained Teddy. 'You start off being irritated by my cool wisecracking, but you end up grudgingly respecting me.'

Maya realized that – annoyingly – this was dangerously close to the truth. 'We'll see,' she replied, smiling. 'Biscuit?'

'Ooh, lovely.' Teddy took two at once. 'Right,' he explained, through an oaty mouthful, fountaining crumbs on to the shoebox, 'we've been staking out the hospital for the past week. We know who the guards are that Lilith's put in place to keep an eye on Maya's dad.'

'We know where they live,' confirmed Bea, tapping at her laptop, 'and we know what time they come on and off shift.'

'So . . . how do we get past the guards?' Maya wanted to know.

'Rule five of spy-slash-secret-mission planning,' explained Teddy. 'There's always a moment where the cool wisecracking one looks all enigmatic and says, "Ah . . . that's the clever part."'

'O . . . K,' Maya said, looking at him blankly. 'So, sorry – how *do* we get past the guards?'

Teddy tried to look enigmatic but actually just ended up grinning. He was so pleased that she'd set up his next line so neatly.

'That . . .' he said smugly, 'is the clever part. Grab Bea's Dream Logbook, and turn to the page with the picture of a cool guy dressed as a pirate.'

*

General Pheare stayed up late that night, watching his favourite programme. It was called *Shark Fishing with the Special Forces* and featured . . . well, you can probably picture it for yourself, can't you? But when he eventually went to bed, something very peculiar started to happen to his dreams.

DREAM LOG

Creator: Pheare, G.

28 May, 11.02 p.m.

Pheare dreamed he was walking through the small terraced house he'd lived in when he was small. He could see the pictures of his grandad on the sideboard, splendid in his army uniform. That was what made him want to join up in the first place, he remembered. In front of the sideboard was the old battered sofa he remembered so well. He used to take the dusty-smelling cushions off it to make forts and hide for hours. Pheare gazed at the dream sofa fondly, until something extraordinary happened (luckily, as this section was in danger of falling foul of our Boring Dream Guarantee).

This is the thing that happened:

An enormous cow leaped out from behind

the sofa and ran straight at Pheare on its hind legs, screaming at the top of its voice.

'RAAAARRRRGH!'

screamed the cow.

'AHOO! RUFF!

Booga-booga-booga!
Prepare to be cowdlarized!'

'WHAAAAARGH!'

cried Pheare in his dream, in panic.

'The dream cow will get you!' wailed the cow in a scary voice.

'GRAAAAAH!'

Just before the cow reached him, General Pheare woke up in a cold sweat. 'Cow,' he murmured to himself, reaching out for the military-style water bottle beside his bed. 'Cow attack.'

Inside the mattress van, which was parked in the street outside, Maya pulled the Dream Dome away from Teddy's head. '"Prepare to be cowdlarized?"' she queried, raising an eyebrow.

'I had to improvise,' protested Teddy. 'Great cow costume, though, Bea. Thanks!'

'You got it!' Bea looked round from her console, where a screen showed a rotating picture of the cow costume, and gave a quick thumbs up.

'So . . . job done?' Maya wanted to know.

'No way,' said Teddy. 'We've got to make double, treble sure this is going to work. We need to give him cow nightmares several times to make sure this works. When can you sneak out again, Maya?'

DREAM LOG

Creator: Pheare, G.
29 May, 11.39 p.m.

The next night, General Pheare was dreaming he was walking along a beach in the bright sunshine licking an ice cream. Gulls cried overhead and the swoosh of the gentle waves was soft and reassuring. He squinted in the bright light to try and make out an indistinct shape in the sky. Was it some kind of bird? Or a plane, perhaps? Gradually, Pheare became aware that it was a figure dangling from a parachute, dropping rapidly towards the beach. The parachute was striped black and white and, the more he strained his eyes, the more it looked as if the figure beneath it was black and white too.

Suddenly, Pheare's back was doused by a chilly gush of fear. Surely, it couldn't be a . . .

'Skydiving cow!' bellowed the figure, plunging towards him and casting an expanding bovine shadow on the sand. It began to laugh maniacally as Pheare turned and ran away from it.

'A-HA-HA-HA-HA-HA ... COWABUNGA!'

Pheare sprinted away. When he threw a look back over his shoulder, he was horrified to see that the cow was almost on top of him. With a fuzzy thump, it crashed into his back, knocking him headlong in the sand.

Pheare awoke sweating and panicking for the second night in a row, spitting imaginary sand out of his mouth.

DREAM LOG

Creator: Pheare, G.

31 May, 1.02 a.m.

Pheare dreamed he was in the army – something he did frequently. He was at the head of his unit, leading them through a dry, sandy valley. 'Keep your eyes peeled,' he said over his shoulder, scanning the surrounding hills for any possible enemies.

Once again, a cold hand of terror stroked his back. He could make out a black-and-white face staring at him from a rocky outcrop not far away. He turned round to warn the rest of his platoon that they were about to come under attack, and froze.

Instead of a line of soldiers behind him, there was a line of cows in combat gear. 'What the –?' said Pheare to himself, but the cow ahead of him had jumped out from behind the outcrop and was sprinting towards him, screaming a terrifying bovine battle cry.

'COWpocalypse NOW!'

yelled the cow.

And Pheare, abandoning every bit of his army training, fled in utter panic. (Incidentally he had never had any real army training. But he had a book on his bedside table called *Secrets of the Special Forces*, which he knew off by heart.)

Out in the van, Teddy was looking at Maya with an expression of slightly guarded respect as he removed the plastic Dream Dome from her head. 'How did you get all the soldiers to turn into cows as well?' he demanded.

Maya looked nonplussed, her head still half in the dream. 'What do you mean?'

'Well, you were dressed as a cow in the Zoetrope. But I was watching Bea's monitor. In that guy's dream, you made his whole army unit turn into cows as well. How?'

'I just, kind of . . . imagined them that way.' It was so straightforward in Maya's head, she found it hard to explain.

'But . . . you actually took control of his dream,' broke in Bea, swinging round on her chair to face them. 'I've never seen anyone do that before.'

Maya felt her face redden as they both stared at her. 'Sorry,' she mumbled.

'Don't apologize!' Teddy laughed. 'It's one of the most awesome things I've ever seen. I'm just kind of jealous!'

Bea was already scribbling in her notebook. '*Maya seems to be able to influence the Dream Field in real time*,' she said out loud as she wrote. '*She can use her own imagination to alter the dream she's in.'*

'Well, I've always been good at imagining things. Or daydreaming, as my teachers usually call it,' said Maya, sitting back and rubbing her eyes. Considering she'd spent a great deal of time this week in other people's dreams, she felt utterly exhausted. Luckily she was managing to snatch a bit of sleep at school – the previous day she'd pulled her hood right over her head and dozed peacefully right through an hour and a half of double maths. But the excitement of planning the rescue, and the prospect of seeing her dad awake, was enough to keep her going.

'Right, I think we can safely say – mission cow accomplished!' Bea went on. 'And, from what I've just seen, I reckon Maya should lead on our next target. What do you say, little brother?'

'Firstly, the expression is "run point",' huffed Teddy. 'Secondly, less with the "little brother". I'm, like, four minutes younger than you or something. But, yeah, sure, OK. She can give it a go.'

'So, General Pheare is sorted,' said Bea. 'Just one more set of dreams to infiltrate, and I think we're ready.'

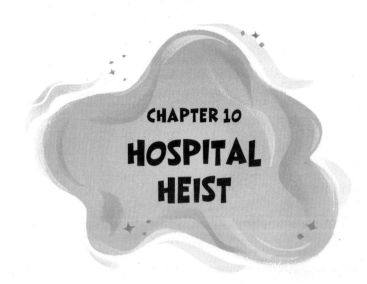

CHAPTER 10

HOSPITAL HEIST

The night was dark and cloudy – in many ways perfect heist weather. Some might say, neist weather for heists. We'd never dream of it, though. Maya sat in the front of the mattress van beside Teddy, who looked nervous and solemn in the glow from the instrument panel as he drove them towards Hagstone Court.

'Is everyone clear on the plan?' said Bea from the control desk in the back. 'We're nearly there. Teddy – you're on the intercom.'

'Roger,' confirmed Teddy.

'Yes,' Bea confirmed, 'you need to talk to Roger on the intercom.'

'Roger, roger,' Teddy replied.

'Maya – you're all clear on the evacuation plan?' Bea checked.

'Operation Tumble? Absolutely, ' Maya answered. 'I think so, at least,' she added quietly.

'You'll be fine,' Bea reassured her, reaching out and giving her arm a reassuring squeeze. 'I'll be standing by here,' she went on in a louder voice.

'Operation Van Nerd,' Teddy mocked.

'That is *not* what it's called,' Bea protested.

'Don't feel bad about being Van Nerd,' Teddy soothed. 'They can provide valuable comic relief at dramatic points during the heist.' He smirked like a smug squirrel who's just inherited a nut warehouse from his wealthy uncle Gordon.

'Right, positions, everyone,' said Bea suddenly. There was a bustle of activity – Maya climbed over into the back of the van and crouched down, as Bea spun her chair round to face her controls, pulling a pair of headphones over her ears.

Maya peered through the windscreen. At the edge of the headlights' glare she could now make out the tall metal gates of Hagstone Court. The high brick walls stretched off to either side.

'Did it never occur to you,' asked Teddy, leaning back in his seat, 'that this looks a whole lot more like a prison than a hospital? I mean, if there's a sliding scale, with prisons at one end and hospitals at the other, this is definitely right over towards the left-hand side.'

Maya didn't reply. When Somnia had offered to pay for all her dad's medical care, she and her mum had just been grateful – it never occurred to her they were trying to keep him safely out of action. Suddenly, the enormity of what they were about to attempt washed over her like a bucket of fish. (We don't know if you've ever had a bucket of fish tipped over you – and, to be quite honest, neither have we. But we imagine it feels a lot like the cold wave of anxiety that hit Maya at that moment. The anxiety didn't smell as bad, to be fair.)

Teddy was pulling the van up next to the gatepost with the intercom. 'Here goes nothing,' he said grimly, winding down his window and pushing the button.

There was a sharp **BEEP** and the metal grille lit up. After a moment a crackly voice replied, 'Hagstone

Court, good evening. State your business, please.'

'Is that Roger?' said Teddy loudly and confidently.

'Err . . . it is, yes. Do I know you?' replied the voice uncertainly.

'We spoke on the phone yesterday,' Teddy went on. 'It's Al here, from Al's Owl Removals. We had reports of an owl infestation, remember?'

Inside Hagstone Court, Roger the security guard furrowed his brow in puzzlement. He did remember having a very strange phone call about owls the previous day, but it had been so weird he'd just assumed it was a dream that had happened when he'd fallen asleep at his desk for a few moments. He pondered. The dream had been so vivid – and now, here was the real-life Al turning up at the gates. It must have been real, he decided. He must have taken the phone call when he was half asleep.

'Drive up to the front entrance,' he instructed, pressing the button to admit them.

'I still don't know why you had to pick something so weird,' complained Bea, as they drove through the smoothly opening gates.

'I panicked, OK?' said Teddy. 'I couldn't think of what to say!'

'Al's Owl Removals, though?' his sister complained. 'You could have picked basically anything but that. What on earth made you think of it?'

'I just like owls.' Teddy shrugged. 'Anyway, I bet none of you could think of a better excuse to get into a secure hospital-slash-prison.'

'You could have said we're here to repair the air conditioning,' suggested Bea mildly.

'Or to restock the canteen?' added Maya.

'Or clean the windows?' Bea went on. 'Check the fire alarms? Repair a fault with the phones?'

'OK, OK, I get it.' Teddy held up his hands in submission. 'Maybe it was a bit spur-of-the-moment. But, look, he bought it! We're in! Time to get in character.' He tossed a pair of blue overalls to Maya and began to struggle into his own. 'Put your over-owls on,' he instructed.

'You did *not* just call these over-owls,' complained Maya as she pulled them on. But she allowed herself a small smile, making sure Teddy didn't see it.

A minute or so later, while Roger the security guard was still trying to work out whether his dream about an owl removal service calling him was real or not, the front doors of the hospital hissed open and two people in blue boiler suits marched in, large black baseball caps pulled down low over their faces. The suits were embroidered with a small owl on each lapel, and the words AL'S OWL REMOVAL SERVICE. Underneath, in smaller letters, was the slogan OWL (WON'T) BE BACK. And on the front of each cap was a cartoon owl with a cross expression. Teddy had really gone to town on the props.

'Evening, sir,' said the first owl operative in an artificially low voice.

Roger scratched his head and peered at him. 'Aren't you a bit young to be an . . . er . . .'

'Owl-removal engineer?' replied the youth. 'Hoo, if I had a pound for every one of my owl clients who'd said that to me . . .'

'How many pounds would you have?' queried Maya from behind him, feeling mischievous and invisible beneath the brim of her cap.

'Well, put it this way,' Teddy replied. 'If owls cost a pound apiece, I'd have enough to stage a full owl baseball game. With owl umpires, owl pitchers, owl backstops and a couple of owls left over to run the PA system and hoot loudly whenever there's a home run.'

The word 'owl' had now been said so many times that it had started to sound really weird. The word 'owl' is quite weird, anyway, isn't it? When you think about it. Try reading this next paragraph out loud in a strong, confident voice. **READY?**

Owl owl owl owl owl

owl owl owl owl owl owl

owl owl owl owl owl owl

owl owl owl owl owl owl

owl owl owl owl owl owl

owl owl owl owl owl owl

owl owl owl owl owl owl

owl owl owl owl owl owl owl.

Owl.

Owl owl owl.

OWL.

Please reassure any parents, guardians or carers that you haven't hurt yourself before reading on.

Now read on.

'Right,' said Teddy, clapping his hands to dispel the slightly weird, owlish atmosphere. 'Time to sort out those owls for you, then. Which way to the attic?'

'Erm, upstairs?' suggested Maya.

'That's right.' Roger looked impressed. 'Keep going up the stairs until you reach the top. That's the attic.'

'That is, literally, the definition of an attic,' agreed Maya as she followed Teddy over to the large staircase.

At this point in any secret mission, the lead heister must touch one hand to their earpiece and mutter the phrase, 'We're in,' in a cool, gruff voice.

'We're in,' muttered Teddy coolly and gruffly, touching a hand to his earpiece.

'Roger,' came Bea's crackly voice in their ears.

'No, he stayed on reception,' Teddy replied, leading them upward.

*

Back at his desk, Roger rubbed his eyes and furrowed his brow, still trying to work out how an apparent dream about an owl removal company had just come true. Part of his brain was slightly disappointed. He had had many dreams in his life, and if one of them was going to unexpectedly become reality, he rather wished it wasn't the one involving owls. Scoring a goal in the World Cup final . . . that one didn't come true. Buying his own private island and installing a race track . . . never happened. Riding a unicorn through the town centre dressed as Wonder Woman . . . nah. But the owl one . . .

'Front desk, come in,' buzzed the voice of General Pheare from the panel on the reception desk. 'Security Control here.' Roger sat up straight. Security Control was where the serious, heavily muscled guards spent the night, checking cameras and making sure nothing odd was going on. And recently their boss, this man Pheare, had been around a lot more as well, constantly prying and asking questions.

'Front desk receiving,' replied Roger, trying to sound as military as possible.

'We've got movement sensors activating on the main stairwell,' said the voice. 'Please advise.'

'Oh, don't worry about that,' Roger answered airily. 'That's just those owl people.'

THERE WAS A LONGISH PAUSE.

'Front desk, please repeat.'

'Owl people,' repeated Roger dutifully. 'Sorting out the – you know . . . the owls. In the attic. They phoned about it yesterday. At least I think they did,' he murmured to himself.

In Security Control, General Pheare took his finger off the intercom. 'Oh, you –' he muttered to himself in frustration, before spinning his chair round.

'INCURSION!'

he snapped to the five burly, uniformed men who were lolling on sofas. (Lolling in the sense of sitting in a casual fashion; they weren't laughing. Just so we're clear. These men rarely, if ever, laughed.)

Within seconds, all six men were on their feet and clomping out of the door.

'SOUND THE ALARM!'

roared Pheare over his shoulder. The last member of the squad slammed his hand on to a large button on the control desk, and red lights set into the walls began to flash.

Maya and Teddy had just reached the fourth floor when the red lights came on. 'They've activated the alarm!' gasped Maya. 'That was quick!'

'I know!' Teddy panted. 'Thought the owl thing would fool them for a bit longer, to be honest.'

'Imagine how much longer it would have held them,' said Maya mildly, 'if you'd said something sensible, like,

"We're here to mend the air conditioning." Or literally anything non bird-based?'

'Look, how many times do I have to owl-pologize?' Teddy answered, chuckling a little at his own joke.

'At least another five times,' Maya told him, deciding it was sometimes just best not to encourage him. 'It's this way,' she continued, pointing down the long passage that led to the wing where her father was being kept. Dimly aware of the stomping of booted feet somewhere below them, they pelted down the corridor.

As the footsteps behind them grew closer, they paused at the shiny keypad that controlled access to the secure wing. 'What was the code?' said Maya. **'Quick!'**

'Hang on, hang on, don't rush me!' Teddy stuck a knuckle in his mouth as he concentrated. 'It took me ages waiting around in that guard's dream to get the combination out of him. And I worked out a really clever way of remembering it.'

'As clever as writing it down?' Maya couldn't stop herself asking.

'Another rule of heists,' said Teddy. 'Never commit anything to paper. Or, if you do, you've got to eat it.'

'Fine,' Maya told him. 'Just tell me the code.

QUICK!'

They could hear that the boots had now started to thunder up the staircase.

'Hens, partridge, lords, lords, rings,' blurted Teddy. 'Got it!'

'What?' Maya paused, fingers poised over the keypad.

'The song, you know . . . the Christmas song,' Teddy told her. 'Hens, partridge . . .'

'Right, so three French hens,' sighed Maya, punching the number 3. 'One partridge. Lords, lords, so eleven,' she pushed the number 1 another four times.

'And rings!' completed Teddy. The door clunked open as Maya hit 5.

'Still think you could just have written it down,' moaned Maya as they raced through, slamming the heavy door behind them. 'Or, indeed, you could just have remembered the relatively simple number 3111115. Anyway, never mind that now! Look for something to jam the door with.'

'Here!' Teddy had grabbed a broomstick from a

nearby cupboard, and rammed it through the handles of the double doors. 'That ought to hold them for a few minutes,' he said grimly. 'Now, hurry up. Let's go and get your dad.'

*

General Pheare led his team at a sprint down the corridor. 'They went this way,' he said, panting. 'This is what we were warned about – they're after the professor in the secure wing!'

'And they're through the security doors,' pointed out the guard behind him as they rounded a corner. 'This is a total worst-case scenario.'

Pheare winced. He was already aware this was a total worst-case scenario. He didn't need someone pointing it out to him. Lilith Delamere would not merely be furious when she found out about this. She would be . . . he searched his brain for the appropriate word and couldn't find one strong enough. In fact, a strong enough word doesn't really exist, so let's make up some new ones, shall we?

Lilith Delamere wouldn't merely be furious when she found out about this . . .

She would be completely and utterly **flandulent**.

KnorSACKED.

Spevulized.

She would throw a **screaming VELP**.

She would launch a **pendiloquence of lundering VOLCASTISY**.

Basically he was in **deep, deep SPLUNGE**.

Frantically Pheare mashed the keypad and pushed the doors, but they wouldn't open. 'Something's jamming them,' he said through gritted teeth.

'We need to get them open,' the guard behind him pointed out. As you may have gathered, Pheare's second-in-command was one of those slightly irritating people who constantly point out obvious problems. 'If the doors aren't open, we can't get in,' he continued.

'Yes, I realize that, thank you, Private Hancock,' replied Pheare tersely, shoving at the doors with all his strength. But the broom stuck through the handles on the other side was an extremely high-quality broom. Built to last. It wasn't giving up without a fight.

'We should help you,' Private Hancock pointed out. 'You don't seem to be able to get the doors open on your own, do you?'

Pheare let out a short bark of rage before beckoning the others forward. Together, they all began pushing and kicking the doors. On the other side, the durable broom began to bend rather worryingly. (Worryingly for Maya and the owner of the broom, that is. This was clearly the broom of someone who cares deeply about broom quality, and only accepts the very best.)

While this broom-based drama was going on, Maya and Teddy had raced towards Professor Dexter's room. Their sneakers squealed like car tyres on the shiny vinyl floor as they pelted round corners. Maya looked over her shoulder as a thundering started up behind them. 'Sounds like they've reached the security doors,' she said tersely, terrified of being caught when they were so close to her dad. They wouldn't get a second shot at this.

'That broom will hold them for a few minutes,' Teddy reassured her. 'Felt like a really high-quality broom, that.' He was, of course, absolutely right. 'How far now?'

'It's just round here,' Maya replied as they squeaked round one final corner. She could see her father's room ahead as the door-hammering din from behind them grew. 'This one,' she told Teddy, turning the handle and leading them inside.

Maya's father lay in bed just as before, the moonlight that shone through the blinds casting white stripes across the blanket covering his legs, with his scarf and glasses neatly folded on the bedside table. The TV in the corner was on, as always, and for a moment Maya expected it to be showing penguin football. But it was something very dull – one of those late-night shows where people sit in chairs and talk at each other while pretending to be friends.

She turned away from the TV to see Teddy already busy with the brakes on the trolley-bed. He touched a finger to his earpiece. 'Bea,' he said softly, 'prepare for extraction. We've got him.'

CHAPTER 11
HEIST-A LA VISTA

We need to begin this chapter with a warning for all broom fans out there. If you are a lover of mops, brooms or other behandled cleaning implements, there is a sentence coming up that you are likely to find extremely distressing. We would like to apologize for this in advance.

READY?

HERE IT IS NOW:

With a sharp, splintering sound, the broom handle parted and the two halves clattered to the floor in a rain of wood chips.

PHEW. That was pretty distressing, wasn't it, broom lovers? If it makes you feel better, we could tell you that the owner of the broom repaired it the next day with a lovely shiny new handle. It wouldn't be true, but we could tell you that anyway. In fact, they threw the broom in the bin. But we won't tell you that, because it would upset you. Anyway, can you please stop going on about brooms? You're delaying the story. Get over it.

Right.

General Pheare and his squadron burst through the door and sprinted up the passage towards the professor's room. 'Split up,' Pheare instructed. 'Block off all available exits. You two, check the lifts by Ward G. You and you, take up positions by the service entrance. Private Hancock, you come with me.'

A couple of minutes later they blundered through the door of the room where, until recently, Maya's dad had been held. The TV still flickered in the corner, but the bed and Professor Dexter were gone. All that remained were the two chairs and a large laundry cart loaded with clean sheets in one corner. 'Right,' said Pheare, looking around swiftly, 'they can't have got very far with him. Come with me.' Turning on his heel, he left the room.

'The professor is no longer in his room, sir,' panted Private Hancock as they ran.

'Yes, I'm well aware of that, thank you,' Pheare replied, stopping briefly to grab his right shoe, which had flapped off again.

'He's been taken,' Private Hancock went on.

'Well, he didn't walk out on his own, did he?' Pheare rounded on him, his frustration boiling over. Lilith would vencularize him if he didn't get her prisoner back. Suddenly, the walkie-talkie clipped to his belt fizzed into life.

'We've sighted them, sir,' came the voice of one of his squad. 'They were heading for the service elevators, but we cut them off. They're in the corridor leading towards Ward B, heading west.'

'Come on, quick,' Pheare ordered. 'This way.' He shouldered through a set of swing doors and through a deserted ward, pushing a loaded metal trolley out of the way as he went. He looked for all the world like a character in one of those medical dramas where they run round hospitals saying things like, 'Get me fifty cc of spleen cream, stat!' Only they're usually dressed like doctors, not soldiers. But otherwise it was very similar. Crashing through another set of doors, Pheare saw a white-coated back disappearing round a corner, pushing a bed.

'It's them!' he yelled, grabbing the walkie-talkie. 'Intruders confirmed, Ward B passageway!' he told the others.

'All units converge!

INTERCEPT!'

Teddy heard the shouting behind him, but he put his head down and pushed the bed as fast as he could towards the main staircase. It wasn't particularly fast because, like all trolleys, it had one slightly rickety wheel which squeaked as if a mouse lived in it, and it kept veering off to the left. But he did his best. The thunder of boots told him he was being chased, but it was only when two burly men appeared in the corridor in front of him that he realized he was trapped.

233

'HALT!'

said a voice behind them. 'Stop pushing that trolley slightly to the left!'

'It's doing that on its own,' Teddy explained. 'Dodgy wheel, sorry.'

'Step away from the bed,' Pheare instructed, pulling out a large white handkerchief and mopping his brow in relief. 'Time to get the professor back where he belongs.' He could now see that the blankets had been pulled right up, so the figure in the bed was completely covered. With a sudden sense of doubt, Pheare flipped back the covers to reveal an inflated surgical glove with a face drawn on it in marker pen.

'That's not the professor,' Private Hancock pointed out, looking over his shoulder. 'That's a glove.'

'**YOU!**' General Pheare snarled at Teddy. 'Where is the real professor?'

'Now, if I told you that,' replied Teddy calmly, 'it would give away the surprise, wouldn't it?'

'GAH!'

Pheare barked in frustration, grabbing the trolley and attempting to tip it over in rage. But unfortunately it was a lot heavier than he'd realized. The trolley teetered on two wheels for a moment before springing back towards him, catapulting the inflated glove right into his face. Pheare reeled backwards as if he were being savaged by a glove-headed monster.

Teddy took his chance. He turned and sprinted off down the passageway, making an extremely irritating sarcastic hooting noise.

'Fight off the glove, sir,' suggested Private Hancock helpfully. 'He's attacking you!'

'Get after that HOOTING YOUTH!'

roared Pheare, his entire career melting in front of his eyes like a snowman in a sauna. 'And the rest of you, split up and cover all exits! **NOW!'**

His squad scuttled away, heading for the main staircase, the service lifts and the back stairs. All the places people could go in and out. But there was one exit Pheare hadn't considered, because it wasn't an exit for people. It was an exit for sheets, pillowcases, duvet covers and towels. Or, to put it more simply, laundry. Dirty laundry.

Remember earlier in the chapter, when we showed you the professor's empty room, and mentioned a laundry cart? We don't just throw in that kind of detail randomly, you know. Let's go back and have another look, shall we?

After General Pheare and Private Hancock ran out of the room, the sheets in the laundry cart began to move slightly. The surface pulsed like a lawn when a mole is about to surface, and after a moment Maya's head popped up. She looked around carefully, and, when she was completely sure the coast was clear, she hopped out and pushed the cart out of the room and down the corridor.

That exit we mentioned was a large metal chute at the back of the cleaners' room. Bags of dirty laundry were tipped down it, and collected in large carts at the bottom. Only right now, there wasn't a laundry cart parked beneath the chute. There was a van. A van with a giant mattress on top of it.

Maya paused at the hatchway, pulling back a handful of sheets to reveal her father's sleeping face. It's not every day you push your dad down a laundry chute. Well, we hope it isn't. If it is, then please stop. Unless he really enjoys it.

'WHEEEEEE!' said Maya, upending the cart and sending the load of sheets and blankets, with her father somewhere in the middle, tumbling down

237

the chute. There was a soft blatting noise from somewhere below, which told her the cartload had hit some kind of soft landing. Steeling herself, she perched on the edge of the chute, and, with a further

'WHEEEEEE!', pushed herself off.

At the bottom, Bea slid out of the driver's seat when she heard Maya's first cry of 'Wheeeeee!' from above. After a moment, the *wheeeeee* was followed by a

WHUMPH

as a tangled mass of sheets thudded into the mattress. Bea climbed up the side of the van and rummaged among them, soon revealing the sleeping professor, looking none the worse for his drop. The second 'Wheeeee!' prompted her to get out of the way, and she dragged him to the side just as Maya made a soft landing beside her, wrapped up in sheets and blankets like a tumbling mummy (Egyptian variety).

*

Teddy dashed down the main staircase as fast as his exhausted legs would carry him. Rounding the corner, he saw the hospital's reception area ahead of him, lit only by the red emergency lights which were still flashing on the walls, casting eerie shadows across the spotless floor. Beyond lay the main glass doors and freedom. But there was a problem.

Standing in front of the doors, arms folded, was the squat, bulbous figure of General Pheare. Even at a distance, Teddy could make out his expression in the reddish lights. It was an expression that said, *Well, well, well. Thought you could escape, did you? Well, think again.*

'Well, well, well,' said Pheare – proving that Teddy

had read his expression accurately. 'Thought you could escape, did you? Well, think again.'

Teddy skidded to a halt at the bottom of the staircase, facing him across the cavernous space.

'Yes, thank you, baby-faced army guy,' said Teddy. 'I can see that you've cut off my escape,' he went on as he began to walk slowly forward. 'In fact, there's no way **throoooooooooough**.'

General Pheare felt a fluttering in his stomach. It was a large stomach, therefore a large fluttering. He frowned. There was nothing to be afraid of here. What had made him anxious? Something the boy had just said to him . . . but what?

'Come no further, I warn you,' he blustered. 'Halt and identify yourself. What have you done with the professor? I know he's still in the building – my operatives have all exits covered.'

'Let's take those points one by one, shall we?' said Teddy smoothly, still advancing. 'Firstly, I said there was no way **throoooooooooough**. Unless you **mooooooooooooove**.'

Pheare took an involuntary step backwards, the

fluttering of panic now expanding upward through his chest.

'Secondly, you asked me to halt. That's going to be a no. What have I done with the professor? Not telling Y00000000000000000U.'

'Come no further,' sputtered Pheare. 'I warn you!'

'But I will identify myself,' continued Teddy smoothly, reaching into his back pocket and pulling out a shapeless black-and-white bundle. 'I'm surprised Y0000000U haven't recognized me already, in fact.' He held out the bundle in front of him with both hands and began to unroll it.

Something about the way the boy was talking had unnerved General Pheare terribly. He tried to put his finger on it; he failed, but then it all became clear . . .

'MOOOOOO!'

bellowed Teddy suddenly and at maximum volume.

'MOOOOOOO!'

He snapped the black-and-white object down over his head, revealing what was in, in fact, a rubber cow mask.

And suddenly the nightmares General Pheare had been having for the last few days flooded back into his brain. He opened his tiny eyes as wide as they would go, which was not especially wide. 'No,' he mouthed. 'No, it can't be. It's not possible.'

'**Ooooh**, but it is,' said the cow, advancing on him threateningly. 'It is I, the cow who haunts your dreams. I am the **NIGHT MOO! RAAAAAAH!**'

Teddy ran forward, waving his arms, and General Pheare broke. Feeling as if his legs had turned into blancmange, he fled across reception in terror, flailing his arms like one of those giant wobbly men who are stationed on the forecourts of car dealerships.

'Looks like a bad case of bovinophobia,' said Teddy into his radio headset as Pheare slammed through a side door and out of sight. Bovinophobia is the technical term for an irrational fear of cows, and Teddy had looked it up online in order to make that exact throwaway remark at that exact moment. As he knew from watching all those films about cool heists, witty throwaway remarks are a very important part of the process.

'Who'd have thought it?' buzzed Bea's voice, and Teddy caught sight of her at the wheel of the mattress van as she pulled round the corner and skidded to a halt on the gravel.

'Did you get him?' he said, running down the front steps. Bea nodded. 'Right, I'll drive,' he ordered, leaping into the cab. 'You head into the back and get ready to wake up the professor.'

The van pulled away with a screech of tyres, disappearing into the night and spraying gravel behind it that winked and glinted in the flashing emergency lights like red sparks.

CHAPTER 12
WAKING DAD

The mattress van smashed through the closed iron gates at the front of Hagstone Court, leaving the sign bearing the slogan HEALTH, SECLUSION, SECURITY spinning on one corner as it roared away.

In the back, Bea and Maya were manhandling the unconscious professor into the NAP chair – no mean feat as the van lurched from side to side and his arms flopped about wildly, hitting them round the face on no fewer than seven separate occasions. Each. Teddy was anxiously looking in his mirror as he drove. 'They'll be after us before long,' he said tersely.

'You could drive a bit faster?' Bea suggested mildly as the professor finally slumped into the chair, still fast asleep.

'Of course, why didn't I think of that?' Teddy shot back. 'And here I was, driving at a relatively slow speed just to build the tension. I'm going as fast as I can, obviously!'

Maya glanced ahead at the dark road unfolding in the headlights. 'When can we wake him up?' she asked Bea, supporting her dad's lolling head.

'We have to divert all the van's battery power to the NAP chair,' Bea replied, 'so we can't do it while we're driving.'

'And right now we really need to be driving,' added Teddy. **'Here they COME!'**

Maya snapped her head round. Sure enough, through the back windows she could make out the double glow of distant headlights.

'I've got a bad feeling about this,' said Teddy through gritted teeth, glancing in his wing mirror and jamming his foot even harder down on the accelerator. It was already flat on the floor, but he was apparently hoping to unlock a secret 'turbo' mode that they had all previously been unaware of.

On the road behind, General Pheare also had his foot flat on the floor. And his black four-by-four was much more powerful than the Flamewoods' electric van – plus it wasn't being slowed down by the weight of a giant novelty mattress on the roof.

It hadn't taken Pheare long to collect himself after Teddy's cow stunt. He had quickly raced through to the back of Hagstone Court, where his car was parked, intent on giving chase. Maybe if he could get the professor back, Lilith need never know this embarrassing little slip-up had ever happened.

He squinted through the windscreen at the red tail

lights and grunted to himself in satisfaction – he was gaining fast.

'We're gaining on them, sir,' piped up Private Hancock from the passenger seat.

'Yes, I'm aware of that, thank you, Private,' Pheare replied. 'I do have eyes, you know.'

'Affirmative, sir,' confirmed Private Hancock.

Pheare rolled his eyes. He'd found the tall, skinny man guarding the back doors and decided on the spur of the moment to bring him along, but he was already regretting his decision.

'He's gaining fast,' shouted Bea, glancing out of the back of the mattress van.

'We need to SHAKE HIM OFF!'

yelled Maya, almost beside herself at the thought that her dad might be taken away from her a second time. And after tonight's heist, there would be no way on earth that Somnia would let them get near him again. 'Should we put Teddy's cow mask on?' she asked frantically, desperate for a way to gain the upper hand.

'What – and moo at them from the back windows?' shouted Teddy over his shoulder. 'Somehow I don't think it's going to work at that distance. But I might just be able to go one better. Hold on tight, everyone! I just spotted something. We're going off-road!'

General Pheare narrowed his eyes as the van, which by now was not far in front of him, abruptly swerved to one side and veered away, bumping wildly as it plunged through a wooden gate and into a grassy field. 'Think you can lose me like that, eh?' he said grimly. 'Well, it's time for a little field trip.'

'That's actually very clever, sir,' said Private Hancock beside him. 'Because a field trip means a trip away, and this trip actually involves you driving into a field.' Pheare snarled. He'd privately been rather proud of that line, but it completely spoils a quip if someone immediately explains it back to you.

'Hold on,' he barked, reaching down and shifting

into four-wheel drive. He spun the steering wheel to follow the red tail lights of the van, which were visible some distance away, bobbing up and down like buoys in a choppy sea, as it careered over the bumpy grass. Pheare's large car dealt with the terrain better, its suspension compensating as he drove over the shattered pieces of the wooden gate. But when his powerful headlights picked out the scene ahead of them, his head reeled. It was, in a very real, completely awake sense, a field straight out of his nightmares. Or, to put it another and slightly less dramatic way, it was a field full of cows.

'AAAAAGH!'

Pheare slammed on the brakes and brought the four-by-four to a skidding halt in an enormous patch of mud. All around him, curious black-and-white faces closed in. The cows, thinking the farmer had turned up to give them an unexpected midnight snack, clustered round the vehicle like bees round a popular bee clothing shop that has just announced all the bee clothes are fifty per cent off. Or, to put it another and less dramatic way, like cows round a car.

'C-cows!' Pheare gibbered.

'The car is surrounded by cows, sir,' confirmed Private Hancock unnecessarily.

Frantically Pheare turned on the windscreen washers, as if the thin jet of blueish water would drive the animals away. One of the cows licked the screen experimentally and snorted, unleashing fresh waves of panic in Pheare's chest. He sat frozen in terror in his seat while moist, kindly cow eyes looked at him from every direction, glinting in the headlights' yellowish glare.

'That ought to hold him for a bit,' said Teddy in a satisfied tone of voice as the mattress van smashed through a second gate at the other end of the field and pulled on to another stretch of moonlit road. 'He's totally surrounded.'

'I do feel slightly bad about using someone's dream against them like that,' mused Bea, half to herself.

'I know.' Maya screwed up her mouth. 'But, to be fair, he was helping keep my dad a prisoner in his own dream. We're kind of giving him a taste of his own medicine.'

'That's twice we've used his fear of cows against him,' observed Teddy in the driving seat. 'I hope we're not milking it.'

'No, Teddy,' Bea told him after a short but intense silence. 'Just, no.'

Teddy shrugged. 'OK, Bea, get the chair ready,' he instructed. 'I'll find somewhere to park, and we should have enough time to divert the battery and power up before Pocket Napoleon back there manages to pull himself together.' Swaying with the motion of the van, Bea worked her way over to her control centre and swung herself into her swivel chair, fingers poised over the keyboard.

'To pull himself together,' Teddy was muttering, 'or, to put it another way, gets himself *udder* control. Udder. Because cows have . . . Oh, forget it.' He pulled the van off the road, into a small car park in a patch of woodland. Maya could see wooden picnic tables among the trees.

'Ready?' Teddy called, reaching down and turning a switch on the dashboard. 'Bea – I'm transferring power . . . now.'

There was a descending hum as the van's engine powered down, and at the same time the lights on the control panels in the back flickered into life. Bea's monitors lit up, and she immediately began typing. 'Maya,' she said as she typed, 'get the dome in position.' Maya reached behind her father's sleeping form and flipped the smoky-grey plastic dome over his head. The glass oval of the CHEESE device on the front was pulsing with its soft golden light.

'All clear, Teddy?' Bea checked.

Teddy opened up one of the van's doors and peered

towards the dark road. 'Nobody in sight,' he confirmed.

'Right,' said Bea, fingers still flying over the keyboard. 'I've got the coordinates to find him in the dream – thanks to you, Maya!' Maya beamed, hardly daring to imagine what was about to happen. 'Let's get a fix on him,' Bea continued. The Dream Dome now filled with the same gentle yellowish light, and words appeared on Bea's main monitor: TRACKING . . . TRACKING . . . LOCATING . . . MIND MESH ACQUIRED.

'Got him!' Bea cried in triumph, moving a slim joystick as she stared intently at her screens. 'Stand by. Extracting in **five** . . .'

Maya felt a chill down her back that was nothing to do with the blast of night air Teddy had just let into the van.

'Four . . .'

She could barely believe it was possible that, after all these wearying weeks, she was about to talk to her dad again.

'Three . . .'

While he was awake, that is.

'Two . . .'

Given the choice, she wouldn't have picked exactly these circumstances – in the back of a tatty van with a huge mattress on its roof, in the woods in the middle of the night, being pursued by the dangerous ruler of a private army with a pathological fear of cows. But, you know, such is life.

'One . . .'

In slow motion, Maya watched Bea reach out for the large green button on her panel marked EXTRACT . . .

'ZERO!'

She pressed it. The golden light inside the dome pulsed – and at once the professor's eyes flicked open. He looked at Maya and immediately his face broke into an enormous grin.

'Morning!' said Professor Dexter casually, as if he'd been asleep for a few hours, not several weeks.

'Morning,' said Maya, mirroring his grin right back at him. 'Any good dreams?'

'To be honest, they went on a bit longer than I'd have

liked,' he replied, pushing the dome backwards off his head. And then he leaned forward and enveloped Maya in the biggest hug imaginable. In fact, you probably can't even imagine it. The kind of hug you wait a full eight weeks for and it still exceeds all your expectations. It was a grade-A hug, truly world class.

'You did it!' the professor congratulated his daughter eventually, releasing her. And Maya realized that spending time with people in dreams isn't half as good as spending time with them when you're all awake.

Professor Dexter was looking around the van, apparently searching for something. Without speaking, Maya handed him his scarf and glasses, which she'd been keeping nearby. The professor balanced the thin wire frames on his nose and wound the scarf tightly round his neck. 'Ah, that's better,' he sighed. 'Didn't feel like myself without those.'

'You didn't look like yourself, either,' said Maya, remembering the hours she'd spent sitting beside him in the hospital.

'So – these are your friends?' her father asked, with an expression of interested surprise.

'Teddy Flamewood,' said Teddy, climbing into the back of the van and saluting for some reason.

'And Bea,' waved Bea from her control panel.

'Flamewood?' queried Professor Dexter. 'So you must be those two terrible twins Julia's always talking about?'

'That's right, yeah,' Teddy confirmed, looking awkward. 'But she's gone over to the other side. She's been helping Lilith.'

'Only because she was threatened, though!' added Bea quickly.

Professor Dexter looked concerned. 'Well, that sounds unusually bothersome,' he mused. 'So, if Julia's not with you, who created this NAP chair?'

'Er, actually, we did, Professor,' Bea admitted. 'We may have, er, borrowed some equipment from Mum's lab, and your blueprints.' She looked as if she were expecting to be told off, but instead the professor clapped his hands in delight.

'How extraordinarily clever of you!' he marvelled, getting to his feet and peering over Bea's shoulder at the control panel. 'This is very impressive!' Maya, behind him, felt a tiny spark of jealousy, but quickly doused it. After all, she was the one who'd found him. She was part of the team. Bea caught her eye and they both spontaneously grinned.

'I can't wait to hear about the rescue,' Professor Dexter said. 'I can't believe I slept through the whole thing.'

'Put it this way, Prof,' Teddy told him. 'It involved dirty duvet covers, broom handles and cows. Lots of cows.'

'That sounds like great fun.' Professor Dexter grinned.

'But we'll have to tell you about it another time,' Teddy went on, pointing out of the back windows.

Maya looked over his shoulder to see headlights approaching. 'Looks like Mr Military has managed to escape from cow-ptivity,' Teddy explained, which was a lot less funny out loud than it looks written down. And even that isn't especially funny.

'Wait a moment,' said the professor as Teddy climbed back into the driving seat. 'Do you mean to say you've been driving the van all this time?'

'Erm, yes,' said Teddy doubtfully, also expecting to get a ticking off.

'How very resourceful of you!' said the professor, beaming. 'Most impressive!'

'Thanks,' said Teddy, relieved. 'OK, Professor – buckle up!' He flicked the switch to divert battery power back to the engine. The headlights flared back into life, illuminating the trees all around them. 'We're not out of the woods yet!' He slammed his foot on the accelerator and spun the wheel, sending the mattress van doughnutting around the clearing. They drove out on to the road just ahead of the huge black four-by-four – Teddy could clearly see Pheare's furious face break into a sinister smile. There was no way they could get out of this one, his smug expression told them.

'We have to try and slow him down!' yelled Teddy. 'Find something to throw! Anything!' Bea and Professor Dexter began scrabbling around in the back of the van for anything expendable, but Maya paused, furrowing her brow in concentration and muttering to herself.

'How about this?' Bea suggested, picking up a large empty plastic bottle. She threw it out of the back doors, where it hit Pheare's windscreen with a dull plunk before ricocheting off into the night.

'That did not appear to slow him down,' Teddy observed, watching in the rear-view mirror. 'And that was my water bottle – I've been refilling it for months.'

'Yes, yes, very green of you,' said Bea, rummaging for other possible projectiles. 'But this is saving the world in a slightly different way. Maya!' she shouted suddenly. 'Don't you dare throw that!' Maya had grabbed Bea's Dream Logbook from beside the control panel and was flicking through it feverishly, still muttering.

'In case you hadn't noticed, we're being chased right now!' yelled Teddy over his shoulder. 'It's not the ideal time to settle down for a nice relaxing read!'

'Wait!' The professor was holding up a hand. 'Don't distract her! I think she may have had an idea.'

As he was closest to Maya, he'd been the first to overhear what she was saying quietly to herself: 'What if? What if? What if?'

'Any sentence that starts with those two words is usually an extremely useful one, I find,' mused her father.

'Look!' said Maya suddenly, folding back the notebook and stabbing her finger at the page. 'Dad! Look at this!'

She was pointing at a diagram of the dome of the NAP chair. Beside it, Bea had made a series of neat notes: *The NAP chair allows us to enter the Dream Field from our own reality. But what if it were possible for the technology to work in the other direction? What if we could bring things out of dreams into the real world? What if we reversed the CHEESE polarity?* **TO BE INVESTIGATED FURTHER**, she had concluded in bold capitals.

Professor Dexter was reading along with her. 'Brilliant, Maya!' he said. 'Why on earth did that never occur to me? Bea, you're a genius!'

'Erm, thanks,' replied Bea, who didn't know which page they were examining. She was looking anxiously out of the back windows at Pheare's headlights.

'What's going on back there?' wailed Teddy. 'Why have you all stopped throwing things and just started complimenting each other? It's no help whatsoever! And what are you doing with *that*?'

In the rear-view mirror he had seen Professor Dexter wrench the plastic dome from the NAP chair, still attached to its thick tangle of wires and cabling, and examine it carefully. 'However did you make this?' he asked. 'Your own version of my Dream Dome?'

'Found it in a skip,' said Teddy proudly.

'How wonderful!' the professor congratulated him.

'You can't throw that at them!' bellowed Bea frantically. 'It took me weeks to build that!'

'I'm not going to throw *this*,' the professor replied calmly. 'That would be criminal! But we might be able to make something to throw. Maya has pointed out an idea in your notebook that is, if I might venture, perfectly brilliant.'

'Oh,' said Bea, leaving her post at the door and working her way towards them, rocking with the wild motion of the van as it careered down the deserted road. 'Well, thanks. Any chance of, you know, doing it quite quickly, though?' Behind her, the lights from Pheare's vehicle cut through the night like the eyes of some threatening, pursuing monster.

'Reversing the polarity . . .' mused the professor, detaching a panel from the side of the dome and examining the wiring. 'That's what you wrote. What if it really is possible to bring something out of a dream? Some small portion of the Dream Field which we could . . . well, throw at someone, to put it simply.'

'WHOA!'

Teddy was listening intently from the driver's seat. 'Are you talking about – a **DREAM grenade**?'

'Well, no.' The professor had detached two wires and was twisting them together. 'I wouldn't quite use that word – that makes it sound rather violent. I theorize that it would be more like a small – erm, I suppose "explosion" is the most appropriate word. A small explosion of dream energy, which you can launch as a hand-held projectile.'

'You have just,' Teddy pointed out, 'given more or less the dictionary definition of the word "grenade" – apart from the dreams bit.'

'Well, yes . . .' The professor had finished his rewiring and was now carrying the dome over to Bea's control area, where he plugged it into a thick cable. 'But I'm sure we can think of a less . . . *angry*-sounding name for it. Teddy – we'll need to divert power back to the CHEESE,' he called.

Teddy glanced over his shoulder. 'You're kidding! The rate he's gaining?'

'Teddy!' urged Bea. 'Do it! It's our only chance.'

'OK . . . get ready,' said Teddy resignedly. 'Here goes nothing.' He flicked the switch once again, and immediately they were all jerked off their feet as the van slowed down. The control unit in the back began to light up, and the professor scrambled to his feet.

'So, you're diverting power from the central unit into the CHEESE?' Bea asked. 'But reversing the energy direction?'

'Yes, just as you suggested in your rather wonderful notebook,' the professor said, golden light illuminating his face as the dome began to activate. 'We should be able to pull a small part of the Dream Field out into our reality. It's certainly an intriguing concept. Let's find out, shall we?'

He turned the Dream Dome upside down, reaching over with the other hand to push a button on the keyboard. The dome filled with light, but Maya could see that it looked different. It swirled sluggishly, almost like glowing soup. (If you're ever offered soup that glows, don't eat it. Just a quick life lesson while we're on the subject.) And, instead of the rich gold of the normal dreamlight, it was shimmering with a rainbow of different colours.

'Fascinating!' exclaimed the professor, the iridescence reflecting from his glasses as the light slopped to and fro with the rocking of the van. 'It appears to have formed a kind of plasma – a thick gas – look! And if your theory is correct,' he continued, 'I should be able to do this.' He dipped his hand into the glowing mass and pulled out a trail of the rainbow vapour. Balancing the upturned dome on his knees, he used both hands to roll it into a ball – looking for all the world as if he were making a snowball.

'So – that's a dream?' breathed an awestruck Maya.

'Well, a small part of one, yes,' the professor clarified. 'A mini-dream, if you like. A dream nugget. A tiny, condensed ball of dream energy that should –'

'LOOK OUT!'

yelled Teddy. There was a huge jolt as the black four-by-four slammed into the back of the van. Now they were coasting with no engine power, Pheare had quickly

266

caught them up. Everyone in the back of the van was thrown to the floor, the professor flinging the ball of dream plasma up into the air as he rolled over on to his back.

'CATCH IT!'

he cried as it reached the top of its flight. Maya, quickly scrambling to her feet, made a dive and grabbed the ball in both hands just before it hit the floor.

'Well held,' her dad congratulated her as he too struggled upright. 'Now, quickly. What kind of dream shall we make this into? What could we possibly imagine that would slow them down?'

'Nails?' shouted Teddy from the front. 'Something to puncture their tyres – that stinger thing you see on police TV programmes?'

'Yes,' said the professor, 'I was thinking along similar lines – or a barrier to block the road. Which is why I am probably the worst possible person to answer the question.'

'Why?'

'Because of my boring, unbendable adult imagination, of course. I'm going straight for the obvious solution, and that just won't do. Maya, why don't you have a go? Remind us how to be fun. Think of the most incredible, creative thing you possibly can to slow our pursuers down.'

'Remember the Dream Bandits' motto!' urged Bea. 'What if?'

'Oh, that's your motto?' asked the professor mildly. 'Mine too. Excellent motto.'

Maya felt paralysed for a moment; it was a lot of pressure all of a sudden, after what had already been a fairly fraught night's work. But then, seeing her dad looking at her with an expression of quiet confidence, her brain-fog cleared. This was imagining – it was what she *did*.

'I've got an idea,' she said – a little uncertainly. 'It might be slightly, uh, weird, though.'

'Weird,' her father told her, 'is exactly what we're after. Because weird is extremely hard to predict. We love weird. Hold on to that weird thought, now. Imagine it as vividly as you can.'

'OK,' said Maya, imagining with all her might as her father touched a button on the Dream Dome. 'What if . . . that car chasing us turned into . . .'

Suddenly a tiny golden spark shot out of Maya's forehead and into the ball of thick gas. It glowed and swirled, and she felt a curious prickling sensation in the front of her brain.

'I can't wait to see what you've imagined,' said the professor proudly. 'If you'd like to hold the back door open, Beatrice, then – as I believe the popular expression runs – here goes nothing.' And as Bea clung on to the doors, he launched the glowing, rainbow-coloured ball out into the night with a slight **WHUMPH**.

The ball cast an eerie light in the darkness, then hit the windscreen of Pheare's car and splatted out across the vehicle like a giant, multicoloured firework. One of the really big ones that they save for the end of the display. And suddenly, Pheare wasn't driving a giant, imposing, black four-by-four any more. He was driving a small, rickety green-and-yellow clown car, his large knees comically stuck up around his ears and his arms bulging out of the sides. His head, which was poking out of the top, wore an expression of confusion. Well, it would do, wouldn't it?

'Our car has transformed into a clown car, sir,' said Private Hancock helpfully, poking up beside him.

In the van, the professor was clapping his hands with delight. 'Oh yes, indeed! Brilliant, Maya. Quite, quite brilliant!'

'How did you do that?' asked Teddy, nonplussed, as he redirected the power to the van's engine and they began to rapidly pull away from the clown car, which was now emitting a comedy **honk, honk** noise. Just before they turned the corner and left it behind completely, Maya saw all its doors fall off.

'I just thought, what's the best way to stop them

chasing us?' she told Teddy. 'And I thought, what if they were driving a clown car? You know, we'd be faster than that. And it would be funny.'

Bea Flamewood was staring at the professor with an awestruck expression. 'Did we just invent a way to bring dreams to life in the waking world?' she asked him.

'Do you know, Bea,' the professor replied, looking slightly taken aback, 'I think you did.'

CHAPTER 13
THE MATTRESS FORT

Julia Flamewood had had a bad day at work. Not just the ordinary sort of bad day, where you spill your cup of tea all over the computer, or the canteen's run out of sausage rolls. A *really* bad day. The sort of day where your crazed boss forces you to work on a secret project to hijack everyone's dreams and replace them with boring images and the occasional advert. Plus the same boss has threatened your family. That bad. Makes the whole sausage-roll thing seem kind of trivial, to be honest.

Julia, feeling powerless, exhausted and close to despair, arrived home to find the mattress showroom in darkness. Unlocking the door, she reached around for the light switch, but when she flicked it nothing happened. Frowning, she **jiggled** it backwards and forward a few times.

(Side note: this is completely pointless. If a light switch isn't working, it's because of some kind of electrical fault. You can't shame it into action by switching it on and off again several times. It isn't going to suddenly say, 'Oh, sorry, that's my cue, isn't it? I was miles away,' and turn the lights on for you. See also: pressing the lift-summoning button several times in a row, or asking a politician a question. Save your energy.)

Julia looked out across the deserted showroom, the empty beds looking rather eerie in the dim twilight. The large double doors at the back of the warehouse were open, and through them glimmered a faint light. She smiled slightly. Perhaps there was a power cut, or a problem with the fuse box. Matt, or, more probably, Bea, would be back there trying to fix it.

But when she walked through the warehouse doors, she realized the source of the light wasn't a fuse-fixing Bea. It was coming from a large mattress fort that had been built right in the back corner, beside the line of parked vans. The fort was as big as a good-sized room, standing two mattresses tall and two wide. And, through a small opening at one end, the soft golden light was spilling.

Ever since they were small, Teddy and Bea had loved building forts in the warehouse, but never on this scale. Frowning, Julia peeked her head through the doorway, waiting for her eyes to adjust. There was a lantern inside, placed on a large table. And in front of it, cast into silhouette by its glow, a figure was sitting cross-legged in a chair. Julia gasped. It was too big to be either Bea or Teddy. And her husband didn't make a habit of hanging out in mattress forts – grown men often don't, which is actually a pity, when you think about it. For a moment she thought that Lillith must have come back to threaten her again, but then she caught a glint of light reflected from large, round, wire-rimmed glasses.

Julia took a hesitant step forward. 'D-Dexter?' she said in a half-whisper.

'Yes, here I am,' said the cheerful, calm voice of Professor Dexter. Julia broke into a huge smile of relief, the desperation and sadness she had been feeling burning away like morning mist in the sunlight. Dexter had escaped. She didn't have to give in to Lilith's threats any more. *This* – she thought to herself – *finally, is the turn of the tide.*

'I'm so pleased to see you!' she blurted out, rushing to the chair and taking his hands. 'And I'm so, so sorry. How did you escape? I mean, I'm delighted you did, but . . . how?'

'Ah, well.' In the dim light she could see Dexter

glance behind her. 'I'm very pleased to say that I had a bit of help from some very clever people.'

Julia spun round to see Teddy and Bea standing at the entrance to the mattress fort, along with a younger girl with short, messy blonde hair and a coat with a large furry hood. 'Meet the Dream Bandits,' said the professor with a smile. 'You know two of them, I believe. The other is my daughter, Maya.'

'I don't understand,' said Julia faintly, backing up to the table and sinking down to the floor.

'Pretty straightforward, Mum,' explained Teddy brightly. 'I overheard Lilith threatening you. So Bea and I hacked your computer, stole all your work files, borrowed one of Dad's vans and built our own NAP chair in the back. We tried to locate the prof in his dream but we couldn't, so we had to recruit a new team member.'

'Nice to meet you, by the way,' said Maya, waving.

'Maya found the prof,' Teddy continued, 'as well as discovering that their scraggy old cat appears whenever she's in the Dream Field. That's not strictly relevant, but it's cool. So once we got a fix on him – the professor, not the cat – we broke him out of that dodgy hospital-slash-prison, woke him up, and here we are.

BISH,
BASH,

and, not to put too fine a point on it,

BOSH.'

'And that's what you call "pretty straightforward", is it?' asked Julia Flamewood weakly, rubbing her eyes.

'Well, I'd love to hear something complicated, in that case.'

'I rather suspect you may be about to get your wish, Julia,' said Professor Dexter. 'Because, if you would be so kind as to tell us what Lilith Delamere is planning to do with my dream technology, I think we have a rather complicated task ahead of us.'

'Which is,' added Maya, joining them at the table, 'to break into her headquarters and stop her dastardly plan.'

'Yeah!' Teddy cheered. 'Heist number two! And this is the big one!'

'So, Mum.' Bea sat down beside her mother. 'You're our spy on the inside, now. What's happening inside Somnia? What's Lilith doing?'

*

What Lilith Delamere was, in fact, doing at that precise moment was screaming. She was doing it very enthusiastically, right into General Pheare's face, from a range of approximately eight centimetres. It was quite difficult to make out exact words among the scream but they were there.

'What do you mean?' she was screaming, at a pitch and volume that would have made bats clutch their sensitive little bat ears in pain if there had been any bats present. 'COWS?!'

'They're large, milk-producing quadrupeds, ma'am,' began Private Hancock, who was standing in the doorway.

'GET OUT!'

Lilith shrieked at him.

'OUT OUT OUT,

KEEP GOING OUT

UNTIL YOU ARE
ALL THE WAY OUT,

AND STAY OUT!'

It came out as more or less one long shriek but, again, luckily we're here to translate for you. Private Hancock scuttled away.

Lilith stepped back from Pheare and collected herself a little. He had shuffled into her office with an air of embarrassment hanging around him like a bad smell. Lilith had started screaming at him almost the moment he'd started explaining what had happened at the hospital the previous night, and she had hardly stopped screaming since. The explanation had taken a full twenty-five minutes and her throat now felt as raw as a freshly vinegared graze. Worst of all, she was conscious of the portrait of her father glaring at the back of her neck. She could feel his disapproval almost physically, like a blast of heat. *So, you let him escape, did you?* She could imagine Doctor Damian Delamere sneering at her. *I always knew you weren't cut out for this.*

She slumped into her chair and rubbed her eyes. Once again she had hardly slept the previous night. And she was so close to activating her invention – to wiping out the bad dreams that kept her from resting. And not just for her, but for everyone. Nobody would be troubled by nightmares ever again.

'So, just to recap,' she said to General Pheare in a dangerously quiet voice, 'you have allowed the professor to escape. One of our very expensive pursuit vehicles has now undergone a clown-car conversion. Professor Dexter may even be awake by now. And if he learns of our plans, he's bound to try and stop them. Is that more or less accurate?'

Pheare nodded, too embarrassed to speak.

'Well, it's clear,' snapped Lilith, 'that we need to activate the Clean Sleep device as soon as possible. Bring Doctor Julia Flamewood here, immediately.'

'Ah, yes.' Pheare tugged uncomfortably at his collar. 'That's another thing. Doctor Flamewood didn't report for work this morning.'

'**WHAT?**' said Lilith. It's only a short word, and one that doesn't often get much attention. But Lilith Delamere managed to infuse that single syllable with so much scorn and anger that it felt to Pheare like he'd been slapped round the face with a medium-sized office block. This didn't make the next thing he had to say any easier.

'Ahem,' he began nervously. 'Yes, it seems that Doctor Flamewood's two children were behind the rescue. Accompanied by the professor's daughter, Maya.'

'Maya Clayton? The girl I told you in no uncertain terms to keep a very close watch on?' asked Lilith, now shaking with rage as if she were sitting on a washing machine full of bricks during the spin cycle.

'That's her, yes!' confirmed General Pheare brightly.

At this point, Lilith Delamere started screaming again.

*

'So she's planning to wipe out dreams completely?' asked a horrified Maya.

'Well, to replace them with her own versions, yes,' Julia confirmed. 'For some reason, she seems absolutely terrified of dreams.'

'I should have seen this coming.' Professor Dexter was twirling the ends of his scarf distractedly through his fingers. 'I should have seen the danger signs as soon as I unveiled the CHEESE to her.'

'You really should think about another name for that device,' Teddy cut in.

'The first thing she said,' Dexter recalled, 'was

something about wiping out bad dreams. Why didn't I pay more attention? My invention was never supposed to be used to banish dreams. It was to understand them – to marvel at the power of the human imagination.'

'Well, I think we can agree that Lilith has got to be stopped,' Maya said firmly. 'Dad, you invented the technology. Doctor Flamewood, you've helped Lilith develop this crazy dream-stealing machine, whatever she calls it.'

'The Clean Sleep,' Julia confirmed.

'Why are scientists so bad at making up names for things?' complained Teddy. 'It sounds like a mop. Should be called something cool, like the Thought Thief or the Nightmare Nicker.'

'Let's stay focussed, shall we?' urged Bea. 'Tricking our way into the hospital was one thing. Getting inside the Heptagon is going to be an entirely different kettle of kippers.'

'Excellent,' grinned Teddy. 'I do like a challenge.'

'If we can get inside,' the professor told them, 'then I can disable Lilith's device. But security will be on high alert.'

'Lilith basically has her own private army,' continued Julia, 'run by that maniac who calls himself General Pheare. And we're on our own.'

'What about Dad?' Teddy wanted to know.

'If we wanted to sell Lilith a mattress, he'd be our first port of call,' said Julia with a smile. 'Invading her lair . . . maybe not so much. No, I think it's the Dream Bandits versus Somnia Incorporated.'

'Awesomeness,' replied Teddy, eyes shining with excitement. 'I like the sound of those odds.'

*

And so, over the next week, they planned for the endgame, as Teddy insisted on calling it. This time, to stay away from prying eyes, the mattress fort hidden away in the back of the warehouse served as their secret headquarters. And this time, Maya insisted that she was in charge of model-making. When they'd planned to infiltrate Hagstone Court, they had only had a cardboard box to work with. Now, thanks to Maya's artistic skills, they had a detailed scale model of the Heptagon made neatly out of white card. It even showed the high wall round the edges, though Teddy had slightly spoiled the effect by strewing the model gardens with empty drinks cans and biscuit wrappers. An additional rule of heist planning, he explained to them, is that you need to snack. A lot.

Professor Dexter felt it was too risky for either him or Maya to go home – Lilith was sure to be watching their house carefully. But one good thing about hiding out in a mattress and bedding showroom is this: there's never a shortage of places to sleep. There was a very emotional video call with Maya's mum, though. As you can imagine, there was quite a lot of explaining to do.

'It will all be over in a few days, Tess, I promise,' said Dexter into the phone. 'But until we've stopped Lilith, I can't tell you where we are. Wait until you see the Dream Field, though. It's wonderful!'

'Just promise me you won't do anything dangerous,' Maya's mum pleaded. 'And I still don't understand the part where the cat started talking to you.' But at that moment Teddy called them away.

'Come on, Claytons,' he shouted from the other end of the mattress fort, where he, Julia and Bea were gathered. 'We still haven't worked out the whole distraction part of the plan!' And Maya and her father had a perfect excuse to wrap up the call and avoid any more explaining.

'Right,' said Teddy, when they joined the others around the table. 'So let's try and crack this. We need to get the professor all the way to the centre of the Heptagon, here.' He used a pencil to point at Maya's model. 'But the security systems will be primed to spot him.'

'So we need to get in there first to prepare the way,' added Maya, feeling very brave and secret-mission-esque.

'But how are we going to take on their security forces?' asked Teddy. 'That guy Pheare's basically got a private army – plus some pretty hardcore vehicles. Apart from the one we turned into a clown car, that is.'

'AH-HA!'

Professor Dexter clapped his hands together. 'Pre – not to put too fine a point on it – cisely, Teddy. One of them is now driving a clown car, thanks to Maya's wonderful imagination.' He sat back, smiling.

'The prof and I have been talking this over,' said Bea, flicking through a notebook filled with diagrams and her small, neat handwriting. 'Remember, we have a weapon that Lilith knows nothing about: Phantasma Plasma.'

'What on earth is Phantasma Plasma?' Teddy shot back, stung that there was a part of the plan he wasn't up to speed with yet.

'That's what we decided to call the prof's invention,' replied Bea. 'The stuff we used to take Pheare out of action.'

'Oh, the Dream Grenade stuff,' Teddy realized.

'Yes, as I explained in the van, Teddy, I think there's a more appropriate name for it,' Professor Dexter cut in. 'Phantasma Plasma is a way of creating a temporary mesh between the waking world and the Hypnagogic Field, you see . . .'

'You throw it at stuff and it creates mini-dreams,' Teddy interrupted. 'No need to go all technical on us. Sounds like a fairly useful way to get security off our backs, right?'

'Indeed it does,' the professor went on. 'Remember, too, that there is a huge dream energy generator right in the middle of the Heptagon. If we can use that to create lots more dream energy, then we could flood the whole place with it.'

'And create as many clown cars as we want!' said Teddy excitedly.

'Clown cars, or whatever you like,' the professor told him. 'The only limits would be your own imagination.'

'So, can you make Lilith's machine do that?' Bea demanded.

'I think so, yes,' he replied. 'I can engineer a circuit to use some of its power. Then, if one of you can slip in and insert that into the, er, Clean Sleep device, that should create enough of a distraction for Julia and me to get into the Heptagon ourselves.'

'And shut it down completely!' Maya finished excitedly.

'Precisely!'

'I'll go in and plant the circuit,' said Bea. 'It'll be nice to get out of the van for once.'

'What do I do, then?' Teddy wanted to know – sounding a little whiny, if we're being honest.

'Well, you and Maya need to create a distraction, so Bea can get in unnoticed,' the professor explained.

'OH, COOL!' exclaimed Teddy, the smile retaking control of his face. 'So we go in there and create a bit of havoc? Excellent!'

'A bit of havoc would answer very nicely, yes,' confirmed the professor.

'Dream havoc, perhaps?' asked Maya suddenly.

'You have the expression of someone who's just had an idea,' Teddy told her.

'I think I have,' said Maya. 'What if . . .' And she cupped her hands round his ear and whispered for a few moments. As she did so, Teddy's face lit up like a lighthouse that is staffed entirely by giant glow-worms.

'Maya has just invented the coolest thing in the history of the entire world, ever,' he told the others. 'But we're going to need some equipment, including a few more of those CHEESE devices.'

'I've got plenty of hardware upstairs,' said Julia Flamewood. 'So I reckon we can sort more or less anything. What's on your mind? What do you think we'll need?'

Teddy stood up and considered the cardboard Heptagon on the table between them. 'Water pistols,' he said decisively. 'Lots of water pistols.'

CHAPTER 14
HAVOC AT THE HEPTAGON

The twin glass doors at the front of the Heptagon's reception area hissed smoothly open to reveal Teddy and Maya standing in very dramatic poses, each holding a large yellow-and-orange water gun. On the top of each plastic rifle a small golden dome pulsed with soft light, and a curly black wire led from the back of each gun to an orange band fastened round their head. Basically they looked cool – that's what we're going for here.

'"Heptagon reception" is hard to say,' complained Teddy. 'I keep wanting to say '"Heptagon receptagon".'

'But that would be ridiculous,' Maya countered.

'Don't you mean "ridictagon"?'

'I most certainly do not.' Maya sniffed. 'Can you please try and focus? We're supposed to be creating a diversion, not making up bad tongue-twisters.'

'Sorry,' said Teddy. 'Bit nervous, actually. I've never invaded a huge, imposing corporate headquarters before armed only with a water pistol.' He waved his gun, making the liquid in the tank on the back of it slop and swirl dramatically.

'Not just a water pistol,' Maya reminded him.

'The Plasma Blaster!' said Teddy proudly. 'Can't believe Bea and your dad actually managed to make these. This is going to be fun.'

'Remember we've only got enough battery power for a few shots,' Maya reminded him. 'So make every one count. We've got to keep them busy while Bea does her thing.'

Far away across the polished floor, the receptionist was watching them from behind his desk. 'Can I help you?' he called finally.

'We're here to destroy Lilith Delamere's invention and save dreams for everyone,' replied Maya brightly.

'Do you have an appointment?' asked the receptionist automatically, before realizing what she'd actually said. 'Wait, what . . .?' His finger hovered over a button marked SECURITY ALARM.

'We don't actually have an appointment, no,' Teddy replied, 'but I'm sure we can . . . dream something up.' And he lifted his water gun dramatically. In his own mind it happened in slow motion, like in a film, but in real life it didn't. If you want to imagine it in slow motion, though, here's the same sentence only slower.

A n d

    h e

       l i f t e d

          h i s

             w a t e r   g u n

        d r a m a t i c a l l y .

Wow, that was just like the movies, eh? For added effect, read it out loud in a really deep voice.

At this point the receptionist pressed the alarm button. Well, you would, wouldn't you? Even though Teddy was holding what was clearly a plastic rifle intended to fire water at people – albeit with a light on top and some sort of attached headset – it was still not the sort of thing you want to see in a corporate setting. Neither was what happened next, which was this:

Teddy pulled the trigger and squirted the nearest object he could see – one of the uncomfortable chairs dotted round the reception area – with a stream of rainbow-coloured Phantasma Plasma. As soon as the dream energy hit it, it began to change shape. The shiny metal legs elongated and sprouted hairs. The hard seat inflated, becoming plump and rounded. And the back of the chair shot upward, stretching

296

into an elegant slim neck topped by a dazzling white head with a long, curved ivory horn.

The chair turned into a unicorn, is basically what we're saying here. But we thought we'd string it out a bit, just to make it more impactful. After all, it's not every day chairs turn into unicorns. Or into anything, for that matter. Generally they stay chairs.

'A unicorn?' questioned Maya.

'Yep,' confirmed Teddy. 'Everyone loves unicorns.'

'He's right, you know,' confirmed the unicorn.

'I challenge anyone not to get distracted from what they're doing if a unicorn turns up,' Teddy continued.

'Spot on once again,' agreed the unicorn smugly.

The receptionist was certainly distracted. Well, he was terrified, if we're being honest. He edged out from behind the desk, eyes popping and fingers pointing. **'It's a – a –'** he gibbered. At that point the doors behind him burst open in response to the alarm and four burly security guards appeared.

'What's the problem?' asked the first of them gruffly. In reply, the receptionist did some more gibbering and pointing. The guard looked over, taking in the kids with water pistols. He was just about to turn back to the receptionist and utter the words, 'It's just a couple of kids with water pistols,' when his brain received a memo from his eyes that had been slightly delayed in transit because of its sheer weirdness. He did a double take so large that it was actually an octuple take, and gazed in disbelief at the large white unicorn that was dressaging across reception towards him.

'What's the matter? Never seen a unicorn before?' asked the unicorn tartly, executing a neat little leap and clipping its rear hooves together. 'Well, it's your lucky day, isn't it?'

The guard gasped. 'What on earth are you doing here?' he said, finally finding his voice.

'Just a bit of modern dance,' replied the unicorn, shimmying to a halt in front of him. 'What did you think?'

'You seem to have imagined a slightly annoying unicorn,' said Maya to Teddy. 'Though, thinking about it, I shouldn't really be surprised, should I? You're a slightly annoying person.'

'I think all unicorns are probably a bit annoying,'

Teddy replied thoughtfully. 'Just because they're so famous these days. I reckon they've started to believe their own hype, to be honest.'

Ahead of them, the unicorn had now segued into a spot of breakdancing, beatboxing with its flexible unicorn lips which, incidentally, are very good for beatboxing. It was, as you can imagine, hard to ignore.

The guards watched with open mouths, which was exactly the point. Teddy and Maya edged round the side of the room while the diversion held. 'Any second now, they're going to come to their senses,' warned Maya, seeing the lead guard furrowing his brow as if trying to remember something.

'Stop those **KIDS!**
SEAL OFF reception!'

yelled the guard suddenly, realizing that his job was to keep the Heptagon secure and not simply to spectate at unicorn dance events.

'How about seal *on* reception?' shouted Maya, quick as a flash, lifting her own water pistol and firing at the large telephone on top of the desk. As the jet of shimmering plasma struck it, the grey phone stretched and morphed into a large seal with a brightly coloured ball balanced on its nose.

'Afternoon, Jeremy,' said the unicorn to the seal, which gave a series of electronic beeps in reply.

'Your seal's still part telephone,' complained Teddy to Maya, who shrugged.

'Still getting the hang of it,' she explained, reaching up and touching the headband which connected the Plasma Blaster to her imagination. 'I was imagining the seal and the phone at the same time – I think they kind of got mixed up.'

'STOP THOSE KIDS!'

repeated the guard, making a run at Maya with his arms outstretched. The other three fanned out, attempting to cut her and Teddy off before they reached the exit.

'I think it's time to take things up a notch,' said Maya breathlessly, dodging to one side to avoid being grabbed.

Teddy nodded in agreement. Standing back to back, they pulled their triggers and sent two huge streams of Phantasma Plasma flying across the room in either direction.

To the left, where Maya's stream landed, the shiny floor tiles immediately began to lift and crack as thick trees and creepers burst upward. Away to the right, Teddy's stream of plasma turned the other half of the floor into a patch of icy-looking seawater studded with ice floes.

'**All units to the reception area – repeat, ALL UNITS!**'

screamed the guard into his walkie-talkie. 'We have an incursion . . . And a unicorn. And a jungle. And the sea. **HURRY!**'

'Would someone answer that seal, please?' asked Teddy, pointing at the seal, which had started emitting an urgent ringing tone.

*

Outside the high white walls that circled the Heptagon's grounds, Bea crouched in a small shrubbery, invisible behind a screen of ferns. She was dressed all in black, even down to a black woollen beanie, from beneath which a microphone stuck out on a wire. 'Mum,' she whispered into the headset. 'Come in, Mum. Do you read me?'

'Mattress Control receiving,' crackled Julia's voice in her ear.

'I'm in position,' whispered Bea, thinking that it was nice not to be left behind in the van for once. 'Let me know when they've started the diversion.' But even as she said it, she could hear running feet on the other side of the wall and two guards shouting to each other.

'Reception area, NOW!
Go, go, GO!'

'Did he say something about a unicorn, or is my radio wonky?'

'We'll find out when we get there, now hurry!

MOVE!'

'Scratch that,' Bea said into her microphone. 'Sounds like the guards are well and truly diverted.'

'All units have been sent to reception,' confirmed her mum. 'You're all clear.'

'Stand by,' said Bea, getting up, 'I'm going in.' Dropping into one of those running crouches that soldiers always seem to do, which really, really make your thighs hurt, she scuttled over to the wall. As she ran, she pulled a small black rucksack off her back and fumbled with the zip. 'I'm at the wall,' she murmured, 'preparing to deploy dream.' She pulled a small, red plastic water pistol from her bag – a smaller version of the rifles carried by Teddy and Maya. Glancing over her shoulder, she flicked a switch and the small CHEESE module fastened to the pistol flickered into life. Concentrating, Bea aimed and squirted a circle of shimmering Phantasma Plasma on to the brickwork. At once, it began to morph and change, becoming white and spongy. Bea pressed a finger into it, then popped it into her mouth. 'Marshmallow,' she said to herself. 'Yum.'

'What's that?' came her mum's voice over the radio.

'I turned a section of wall into marshmallow,' Bea explained. 'I'm going through.' Taking a short run-up, she dived through the circle of goo, emerging on the other side with a very dramatic commando roll. She picked herself up and looked around, licking a few stray bits of marshmallow from around her mouth as she did so. She had emerged on one of the wide, pristine lawns that surrounded the Heptagon, dotted with stunted, over-pruned trees.

Flitting from tree to tree like a confectionary-flecked ninja, Bea made her way to the side of the huge, imposing building.

'I've reached the Heptagon,' she said. 'Status report? Other than the marshmallow being delicious. I know that already.'

'We've hacked into the guards' radio frequency,' her mum told her, sounding as if she were smiling. 'It sounds like Maya and Teddy are keeping them busy. One of them just said something about a unicorn performing a selection of show tunes. You're all clear to proceed to the next phase.'

Fighting down a brief pang of regret that she didn't

get to see the singing unicorn, Bea rummaged in her rucksack once again and pulled out a hard-boiled egg. Placing it on the ground, she aimed her water pistol and drenched it in plasma, concentrating as hard as she could on the dream she wanted to create. With a muffled flump, the egg inflated into a small, puffy cloud, which hovered in the air at knee height. Bea smiled in satisfaction – this was even cooler than a mythical horn-headed horse performing a selection of West End hits. She jumped on to the cloud, which wobbled slightly but supported her weight. *I've always wanted to do this*, she thought to herself delightedly.

'HUP!' she said out loud, and the cloud gave a sprightly little jolt like an extremely fat and woolly lamb, before rising gently into the air.

'Oh, my,' Bea breathed as the cloud rose as high as the roof and she got her first view of the top of the Heptagon. 'You were right, Professor. She's definitely planning something. Something big.'

The entire roof was a forest of tall, thick metal aerials. Each mast was topped with a complicated criss-cross of bars and wires, and these occasionally rotated in unison, pointing this way and that, whirring eerily as they spun. Interspersed among the masts were enormous satellite dishes, their gaping white mouths pointed to the sky. Basically it couldn't have looked any more suspicious, even if there'd been a huge illuminated arrow floating just above it with the words EVIL PLAN IN PROGRESS picked out in multicoloured lights. For a split second Bea was actually tempted to make a similar arrow appear, but quickly decided it would probably just draw attention to her sneaky cloud-riding roof invasion. Besides, she didn't have time. And neither do we, so on with the story.

Steering her cloud with small nudges of her heels, she flew towards a large metal box right in the centre of the roof. It was low and squat, with a grille in the middle.

'Heading for the ventilation shaft,' Bea told her mum over the radio, unable to suppress another thrill of excitement that she actually got to deliver such a dramatic, secret-missiony line in real life. While riding a cloud.

'Good luck,' came the reply. 'It should lead you right

to the main lab.' Back in the van, Julia experienced a similar thrill for similar reasons.

Pulling out her water pistol as she approached the top of the duct, Bea squirted the grille, which immediately turned into a flock of colourful butterflies and fluttered away like confetti in the wind. Steeling herself, she nudged her cloud forward and downwards, drifting softly and cautiously down the wide metal shaft.

*

Let's head back to the reception area and find out how things are going there, shall we? You might not recognize it, though – things have changed quite considerably since we last saw it, just a few short paragraphs ago.

'Hakuna Matata!' sang the unicorn in a warbling falsetto, pirouetting neatly on its two front legs and kicking an approaching guard in the chest with its hind hooves. 'What a wonderful phrase.' All around it, thick jungle plants and creepers now filled the room, the shiny white floor tiles only showing through here and there. From somewhere in the distance the seal phone emitted a digitized version of 'Greensleeves'.

'Sounds like the seal's put someone on hold,' said Maya to Teddy as they plunged through the undergrowth, still trying to keep the guards busy for as long as possible. 'How long do you think your sister will need?'

'She said around twenty minutes,' said Teddy, looking around him at a small clearing among the ferns. 'How long do you think it's been now?'

'Well.' Maya thought for a moment. 'The unicorn's run through a couple of songs from *Matilda*, and now it's started on *The Lion King*. So that must be ten, fifteen minutes' worth at least.'

'Right,' said Teddy. 'We just need to keep them tied up a little longer. How much Phantasma Plasma do you have left?' Maya looked down at her water gun, where a red light was blinking next to a label reading BATTERY WARNING.

'Why can the most brilliant inventors in the world still not make an electronic device with half-decent battery life?' Teddy complained. 'I'm just about out too,' he realized, seeing the red light on his own rifle. 'Oh well,' he decided, 'we'll just have to rely on good old-fashioned running about and shouting for the remaining five minutes, I guess.'

CHAPTER 15
RUNNING ABOUT AND SHOUTING

And so, for the next five minutes, Maya and Teddy ran about and shouted. We could describe it, but it's much more fun to experience it for yourself. This is a book all about imagination, after all. So, after three, let's all run about and shout, shall we? If anyone complains, just tell them you read it in a book and they're stifling your creativity. Blame us, basically.

Right, then. After three, ready?

One.

Two.

ARRRRRGHGHHHHHHHH!

No, stop it, Greg. We said *after* three. Not *on* three. Calm down. Let's try again.

One.

Two.

Three.

ARRRRRGHGHHHHHHHH!

(That's better, well done.)

WAROOOOOGGGGHHHHH.

HARRRRGH!

Flaaaaaaaaaaaaaaarrrrrrrrrgggghhhhh!

This is fun, isn't it? And it's exactly what was going on in the Heptagon's reception area too.

'WAROOOOOGGGGHHHHH!'

screamed Teddy, leading a group of guards on a wild goose chase through the jungle. Although there weren't any geese there – just a unicorn. But a wild unicorn chase isn't a thing, is it? Well, we suppose it is now.

'HARRRRGH!'

said the unicorn, jumping out on the guards from behind a shrub and poking one of them in the cheek with its horn.

'Flaaaaaaaaaaaaaaarrrrrrrrgggghhhhh!'

screeched Maya at the top of her voice, diving behind the bleeping seal on the reception desk and skidding into a hiding place next to a small filing cabinet.

Right, you can stop running about and shouting now. We're going to go and see what Bea's up to, and we all need to be quiet, because it's secret.

*

The main laboratory at the centre of the Heptagon was completely deserted. When the alarm had sounded, it had been completely locked down. The doors were sealed shut; there was absolutely no way for anybody to get inside – unless they were riding a small cloud and had just flown down the large air-conditioning duct in the centre of the ceiling.

Riding her small cloud, Bea emerged from the large air-conditioning duct in the centre of the ceiling and floated silently downwards. She jumped lightly to the floor, giving the cloud a small, grateful pat, as if it were a faithful, plump little white horse, and moved over to the banks of wiring and control panels connected to the large column in the centre of the floor.

Pulling a small screwdriver from her rucksack, Bea carefully removed a metal panel, revealing a jumble of multi-coloured wires inside. Putting the screwdriver behind her ear, she began to untangle the spaghetti of wiring – carefully separating the different colours. 'I've gained access to the main control terminal,' she whispered into her headset.

'Wonderful work!' came the faint voice of Professor

Dexter. 'Now, you remember what to do?'

'Of course,' said Bea matter-of-factly, still sorting the wires. She followed one clump back to the circuit board they were plugged into, rummaging in the rucksack with her other hand and pulling out a small black box with a pair of clips sticking out on two red wires. 'Stand by,' she breathed, 'I'm going to insert our replacement circuit.' Holding her breath, she placed the two clips over two of the wires, squinting with concentration as she double-checked and triple-checked they were in the right place. 'OK,' she said finally. 'I think that's it.'

'Well done, Bea!' the professor's voice crackled in her ear. 'We'll get in position.'

'Preparing for activation,' Bea replied. 'Ten seconds and counting.' She started counting down under her breath as she moved to the main control desk: 'Ten . . . nine . . . eight . . .' She realized at this point she was already at the desk and ready to go. 'Wow, ten seconds is actually quite a long time when you're really tense,' she said to herself. 'Maybe I should have started at five. Oh well, I'm at five now, anyway. Four . . . three . . . two . . .' Her finger hovered over the main switch.

'**ONE,**' said Bea out loud, and flicked the switch downwards.

There was a deep hum as the huge machine in front of her began to operate. Bright lights flashed on and off across the control panel, and Bea could see that the circuit she'd added to the system – still dangling by its own wires – had started to glow with a series of bright colours as the power coursed through it. Then, all at once, a shimmering field of energy began to spread outwards from the machine. It swirled and rippled like a strange heat haze, shining with brilliant rainbow colours like the reflections in a huge bubble.

'It's working,' said Bea delightedly. 'It's working!' The field continued to spread outwards, and Bea felt a strange, warm sensation as it passed over her, as if she'd stepped into a cosy room after playing out in the snow.

'Well, time to test it out, I guess,' she said to herself, screwing up her face in concentration. Immediately, there was a further shimmering in the air beside her and a tall frosted glass appeared, with two striped paper straws poking out of the top. 'Hypnagogic Field activated!' she told the professor.

'You managed to manifest an actual dream?' replied his excited voice. 'What did you create?'

'Oh, just a milkshake,' she told him, taking a sip. 'It's thirsty work, you know, all this infiltrating a top-secret laboratory and rewiring the entire control system stuff.'

'Just a milkshake?' the professor asked, sounding a little disappointed. 'When you could have imagined absolutely anything?'

'Well, not *just* a milkshake,' confessed Bea. 'It's actually a bottomless one that stays cold for ever. Plus, you can drink as much as you want without getting full, and it's the flavour of a different chocolate bar every time you take a mouthful.'

'Fair enough,' conceded the professor. 'Maybe you could make me one of those when we've finished.'

'You're a grown-up,' Bea reminded him. 'You'd probably want something gross like a coffee-flavoured one or something.'

The Dream Field continued spreading, moving out through the walls and along corridors, until it filled the entire Heptagon.

'Teddy, Maya, come in,' said Bea into the radio. 'Mission successful. The entire building is now meshed with the Hypnagogic Field. Anything you can dream up – it will appear. You won't need the Plasma Blasters any more.'

'Message received,' answered Teddy, sounding as excited as a kitten who's just bought its own wool factory. 'Maya – **IT'S SHOWTIME!**'

*

Back in reception, Bea's message didn't come as a surprise to Maya. She had watched the strange, shimmering mirage spread out across the room, and as soon as it passed over her, she felt something against her lower leg. Looking down, she saw that Bin Bag had appeared and was already attempting to hide behind her calves.

'This all looks extremely distressing,' Bin Bag complained. 'There's a complete lack of soft furnishings of any kind. Worst environment imaginable.'

'There's a unicorn, though,' Maya pointed out encouragingly.

'Oh, great,' moaned the cat. 'Someone else who wants to be the centre of attention.'

Meanwhile, Teddy – immediately after yelling, 'It's showtime!' – had decided to turn the entire room into a roller disco. The lights turned different colours and began to flash, pumping music appeared from nowhere, and the guards were all suddenly wearing roller skates. They careened around like pinballs, cartwheeling their arms as they desperately tried to stay upright. Maya, peeping out over the reception desk, was unable to keep herself from laughing as one of them – frantically yelling, 'What's going on? What's going on?' – somersaulted and landed flat on his back.

*

Up in her office on the seventh floor, Lilith Delamere, in frozen disbelief which was rapidly melting into a pool of panic, had been watching the scene unfold on a large monitor. How was any of this possible? Why was her lovely clean reception area now full of unicorns, flashing lights and roller-skating nincompoops? She jabbed a finger at her communication console. 'Pheare! Status report! What on earth is going on?'

'We're . . . we're not sure, sir,' General Pheare's terrified voice replied. 'They seem to be deploying seals and, and . . . possibly balloons.'

The monitor showed that brightly coloured balloons had now started cascading down from the ceiling of the reception area.

'They're not *deploying* them, you idiot!' Lilith shrieked. 'There's a unicorn in there, for heaven's sake! Unicorns don't exist! These are *dreams*! Strange, dangerous, frightening dreams! How are they doing this?' She mashed buttons on her control unit, flicking through different cameras until the monitor showed the feed from the front doors. Standing just outside was a man with unkempt grey hair, wearing a brown checked jacket, with a long stripy scarf wound several times round his neck. As Lilith watched, he looked up and waved cheerfully right at the camera, the light flashing from his large round glasses.

'*Clayton* . . .' Lilith snarled. 'I should have known. This is just the sort of dangerous frivolity he would be involved in.'

On camera, Professor Dexter stopped waving and knocked loudly on the glass doors.

*

'That's my dad!' yelled Maya, rushing across reception, batting balloons out of her path. 'I've got to let him in.' But how would she do it? She stopped and thought for a moment.

Why don't you have a think, too? You can imagine anything you like and it'll appear. How would you open a set of doors to let the professor inside? Got a good idea? So had Maya.

The doors turned brown and knobbly as their glass and steel turned into old, knotted wood. And suddenly they flipped downwards.

'A drawbridge! How delightful!' exclaimed the

professor, stepping across to a brassy fanfare of trumpets. 'I've always wanted to invade a castle by storming over a drawbridge!'

'You're not really dressed for it,' mused Maya. With a **pop**, a highly polished, pointed helmet appeared on her father's head. 'And, really, you should be on a horse,' she added. But before she set about imagining one, there was a clip-cloppage from behind her and the unicorn appeared, cantering merrily through the balloons.

'May I be of some assistance?' it asked, bending its front legs so the professor could climb on to its back.

'Much better,' Maya approved, standing back to admire the spectacle of her dad wearing a silvery helmet and riding a unicorn. It's not a sight you see every day, to be honest. Or, indeed, ever. 'Right,' she went on. 'Time to put a stop to Lilith's evil master plan, I think.'

'I entirely agree,' said her father with a smile. 'Or, to put it another way –' he adjusted his helmet and cleared his throat –

'CHARGE!'

He dug his heels into the unicorn, which bleated loudly in protest but broke into a gallop, popping balloons left, right and centre as it pelted towards the doors beside the reception desk.

'Cats are terrible at rescue missions,' wailed Bin Bag, still looking around for somewhere comfortable to lie down.

'You'll have to be the exception that proves the rule,' Maya scolded him. 'Come on.' And she led him across the reception area in her father's wake.

The professor, charging across the room, with roller-skating guards scattering in front of the galloping unicorn like bestruck skittles, shouted back to Maya over his shoulder, 'The human imagination is the greatest musical instrument in the entire universe. What a shame that, as they grow up, so many people forget how to play.'

*

'PHEARE! PHEARE! GET IN HERE!'

screeched Lilith Delamere into her intercom.

'That rhymed,' panted General Pheare a few moments later as he barged in, hitching up his belt over his podgy tummy.

'What?' she snapped icily.

'You said, "Pheare, Pheare, get in here,"' he pointed out. 'It's like a little poem.'

Lilith pointed to her monitor. 'Our facility has been **INVADED** by Professor Dexter and what appears to be a group of

CHAOS-CAUSING CHILDREN,'

she screamed into his face. 'Our entire project is under threat! You need to take your best troops and stop them! **NOW!**'

'Well, that didn't rhyme.' Pheare huffed, but only quietly. He sensed his boss wasn't in the mood for poetry right now.

'Somehow they've managed to take over our systems and flood the entire building with dream energy,' Lilith told him. 'I've been watching them in the reception area. It seems they're able to bring their own –' she almost choked on the next word – 'imaginations to life.'

'But . . . how on earth are we supposed to fight against all that? Against unicorns and things? They can imagine anything and it'll appear.'

'It'll work for *anyone*, you idiot!' yelled Lilith. 'They're not the only ones with imaginations, are they? So get some soldiers together, track them down and imagine some things that'll stop them. Got it?'

Pheare furrowed his brow in concentration. Suddenly there was a small **pop** and a large sledgehammer appeared in his right hand. His expression cleared. 'Oooh,' he exulted. 'We could imagine, like, loads of really big weapons!'

'THAT'S WHAT I JUST TOLD YOU!'

Lilith shouted. 'Now get down there and

WIPE THEM OUT!'

*

Professor Dexter slowed the unicorn to a trot as he approached the double doors beside the reception desk. A green light blinked and a neighing voice sounded from the speakers: 'Unicorn identity confirmed. Access granted.' Clearly the electronic systems that controlled Somnia's security weren't immune to the flood of dream energy.

'Follow me, and stay close,' the professor told Maya and Teddy as the doors slid open. 'It looks clear ahead, but I don't trust Lilith. She's bound to have something up her sleeve.'

Beyond a set of glass doors at the end of the passageway, Maya could make out running figures. 'There's someone down there, Dad,' she pointed out tersely. Beside her, Bin Bag mewed faintly.

'Imaginations at the ready,' instructed the professor calmly. 'Looks like Lilith's arranged a little welcoming committee for us.' Slowly, they approached the doors and peered through.

General Pheare hadn't wasted any time. He spent a great deal of his life imagining large military machinery, so when he was informed that he could do this and it would actually appear, it felt very much like army-Christmas. The large room at the end of the corridor was now almost entirely filled with a bewildering array of things, every single one of them painted in camouflage colours.

Right in the centre of the room was the very first thing that Pheare had imagined – an enormous tank. He was sitting proudly on top of it, in full combat gear, with one of those olive-green nets draped over his head. To one side was Private Hancock and some of his crack soldiers, positioned behind a line of huge concrete and metal barriers. And to the other side, something that Pheare had imagined at the last minute when he'd heard unicorn hooves approaching and had panicked slightly.

Having imagined a tank and a lot of metal and concrete, he'd rather begun to run out of ideas. But then, out of nowhere, the thought had popped into his head: *What about a squadron of robot super-soldiers?* And, thanks to the Dream Field that filled the building, they had duly appeared. They looked silvery and mean, with huge arms and oversized khaki helmets on their heads. Pheare looked across at them affectionately from the top of his tank. Surely nothing could get past his own private imagination army! He felt utterly unstoppable. (Spoiler alert: he wasn't.)

The glass doors hissed open to reveal Professor

Dexter, flanked by Teddy, Maya and Bin Bag. The professor dismounted from his unicorn, giving it a grateful pat on the neck. The unicorn hooted affectionately in reply before cantering off back towards its indoor jungle.

'Well, good morning,' said the professor evenly, looking around at the soldiers, the huge tank and the intimidating robots. 'Nice to see you all.'

'Stop where you are!' Pheare ordered the three intruders (well, four if you count the talking cat – which you should). 'You're all trespassing. And your little invasion ends right here. Hands up!'

'This looks pretty scary, you know,' muttered Teddy out of the corner of his mouth.

Maya looked sideways at her dad. How on earth were they going to get past this?

'Don't be scared,' the professor told the two of them kindly. 'Just take a look at what these big tough guys have dreamed up. Not particularly ground-breaking, is it? A tank to fight a battle? Not especially original. In fact, it's about as predictable as that angry little man saying, "I'm warning you," any second now.'

'I'M WARNING YOU!'

shouted Pheare at that exact moment.

'Told you,' said the professor, sighing. 'Yes, I don't think there's any reason to be afraid. In fact, I dare say the two of you can imagine something far more ingenious.'

At this point, General Pheare lost patience. He was used to being obeyed – and something about the professor's easy confidence had him thoroughly rattled.

'FIRE!'

he bellowed, slamming an arm downwards in a chopping motion. Maya and Teddy both instinctively ducked as a huge rumbling roar came from the tank's gun. But instead of a shell or an explosion, a jet of thick yellow gushed out of the end, forming a large steaming puddle on the floor in front of them.

'What on earth is that?' asked Teddy, dumbstruck.

'Custard!' came a shouted reply from the other side

of the room. Bea floated into view, riding her small white cloud once again.

'So it is,' said Maya, dipping a finger in and licking it. 'Nice and hot, too. Nothing worse than cold custard.'

'First good thing that's happened all day,' agreed Bin Bag, padding over to a nearby custard puddle and lapping at it greedily.

'Attack! ATTACK!'

screamed General Pheare, furious that his impressive military hardware was being mocked in this way. Plus, he hated custard. We know that sounds ridiculous, but it's true. Some people do, you know. Mostly evil people. They prefer their puddings dry, villains.

'ROBOTS! ATTACK!'

Pheare shouted. The robot soldiers jerked their heads up and began to lumber forward, smashing their metal fists together in fury.

'Now's our chance,' encouraged the professor. 'You saw what Bea was able to do. These tough guys have got pretty limited imaginations.'

'True,' said Teddy. 'I mean, for a start he's only imagined –' he counted quickly – 'ten robot soldiers. Why not, like, a million?'

'I'm pretty tired, though,' complained Maya.

'That's often when the best ideas come,' encouraged the professor. 'I get many of my best ideas when I'm half asleep. And some of them when I'm completely asleep! Time to really delve into your imaginations. It's time to fight fire with . . . fun!'

'I've got something,' said Teddy, diving to one side and squinting with concentration. With a **pOp**, the military helmet atop the nearest robot transformed into a cowboy hat, and it began stomping its foot rhythmically. 'I'm trying to make them line dance,' Teddy explained. 'Give us a hand, Maya.'

The idea of a squadron of line-dancing robots was so amazing that Maya found she was able to imagine it quite clearly straight away. And no sooner had she imagined it than it came to life. Suddenly all the robots were wearing cowboy hats, and the one on the left of the group had produced a banjo from its holster instead of a gun. A large drum appeared in front of its neighbour, and they began to play a toe-tapping country-and-western tune. Soon all ten robots were whirling in time, tipping their cowboy hats and occasionally crying, 'Yee-hah!' in their deep robotic voices.

'Pheare!' crackled Lilith's voice from the walkie-talkie on General Pheare's belt. 'Status report! What on earth is going on down there?'

'The robots are line dancing,' gabbled Pheare, 'and the tank fires custard.'

'What? What are you blathering about, man? Attack them! Drive them away! Now!'

'ATTACK!'

Pheare commanded his soldiers, who had been crouched behind their concrete and metal barriers watching what was going on with frank amazement. But, before they could charge, the barriers turned into large sheets of red cloth.

'Bulls!' gibbered the soldier on Pheare's left. Without thinking, he had grabbed the red cloth – but he could now see that there were, indeed, several large bulls charging at them. The leading bull was playing a stirring Spanish tune on a trumpet.

General Pheare, still mortally afraid of anything cow-shaped, broke and ran, with the other troops pelting after him.

'We've got them on the run!' shouted the professor in triumph. 'Come on! Let's find Lilith and put a stop to this!'

One last soldier, standing firm against the onslaught of bulls, managed to fire one more gout of custard from the tank as they dashed past, but it did nothing more than provide Maya with a lovely sweet snack that made her feel a lot less tired and completely ready for a proper final confrontation. Which is lucky, because that's exactly what's about to happen in the next chapter.

CHAPTER 16
THE DOCTOR'S PORTRAIT

As you'll be aware by now, Lilith Delamere was not an enormous fan of imagination. Her fierce father had drummed it into her that imagining things was nothing but a waste of time. 'If it's not real, you can't sell it,' he used to say to her, 'and if you can't sell it, it has no practical purpose.'

Now, sitting in her office watching her expensive security force being chased by a group of bulls that had been summoned directly from a dream, Lilith realized she hated imagination more than ever. It's one thing to have imagination somewhere out there where it can't reach you – it's quite another when it bursts into your office and starts smashing up the furniture.

On the monitor she saw General Pheare climb down off his tank and slip over in a pool of custard. For a split second the side of her mouth began to curl upward, as if a tiny part of her face were thinking about breaking into something that could almost be mistaken for a smile, but she reached up and pulled it down again with a thin finger.

'You're enjoying this,' said a mean, cold voice from behind her.

Lilith froze in total terror. There was nobody else in the room with her. Nobody except . . .

You know that feeling, when you're convinced there's something behind you but you don't dare turn round, because turning round will make it real? That's exactly how Lilith felt at that exact moment.

'I always knew it would come to this,' the hard, mocking voice went on. 'You thought you had what it takes to run my laboratory . . . messing around with your silly little ideas. It was bound to end this way.'

'What, with a custard-firing tank?' said Lilith, suddenly feeling a strange compulsion to break into giggles.

'With frivolity!' snapped the voice. 'Ridiculousness. Froth. Nonsense. Time-wasting. Silliness. No one has ever accomplished anything with silliness. Nobody. Ever.'

On the monitor, Maya and Teddy had now reached a set of secure double doors that led towards the Heptagon's central laboratory. Maya turned the doors to cheese and Teddy, snapping his fingers, produced several large bread rolls. Lilith again felt that strange tugging at the corner of her mouth as they began to work their way through by pulling off large pieces and stuffing them into the rolls.

'They're making door sandwiches,' she marvelled.

'This foolishness must STOP!'

roared the voice from behind her, at such volume that Lilith unthinkingly turned round. Sure enough, the portrait of her terrifying father had come to life. No longer two-dimensional, it now looked as if the frame had a large, colourful room behind it. And standing in that room was Doctor Damian Delamere, even taller, more imposing and forbidding-faced than ever.

'I can see I'm going to have to take matters into my own hands,' he said icily, stepping forward with one long, black-clad leg, preparing to climb out of the frame.

'NO!' Lilith gasped. 'You can't do that! Stay in your painting!'

'This is now a building where dreams come to life,' replied her father, smiling a chilling smile. 'Nobody said it just had to be the good ones.' And placing his bony hands on the sides of the frame, he vaulted through.

Screaming in terror, Lilith dived for the lift, frantically mashing her finger on the CLOSE DOORS button.

*

'The main lab's just down here,' the professor yelled over his shoulder, leading Maya, Bin Bag, Teddy and Bea down a wide hallway that ended in a huge metal panel studded with bolts.

'What's the combination?' shouted Teddy, darting over to a keypad beside it.

'The building's flooded with dream energy,' the professor reminded him. 'The combination's whatever you imagine it is!'

'Oh yeah!' Teddy's face lit up with delight. He turned back to the keypad, which was now no longer a simple set of numbers, but a much larger panel with brightly coloured images on each button. 'Let me think,' Teddy mused. 'What is that combination? Ah, I know –' he cracked his knuckles and started punching buttons – 'sausage, pineapple, sausage, sausage, Nelson Mandela, soup ladle, cat emoji . . .'

'Excellent choice,' said Bin Bag smugly.

'Sausage, flying bus, sausage . . .' Teddy continued.

'A simple four-digit combination would have been quicker,' Bea scolded him.

'Yeah, but not as much fun,' he countered. 'Nearly

finished. Now then . . . sausage, lasagne, meatballs, raccoon on a jet ski.' He pushed the final button and with a deep rumbling the panel began to slide upward.

'This is it!' the professor told them. 'The central control systems are all in here. If we can shut this down, Lilith won't be able to carry out her dream robbery!'

'Quick, Dad!' Maya encouraged him, as they pelted into the huge lab, with its giant tower of machinery in the middle. 'Shut it down! Shut it down!'

'SHUT IT DOWN!
SHUT IT DOWN!'

screamed a different voice from the other side of the room.

'Weird echo in here,' commented Teddy drily.

'That's no echo,' said Professor Dexter grimly, pointing. 'That's –'

'Lilith!' Teddy, Bea and Maya gasped at the same time, in what will make a very dramatic moment if this ever gets made into a film. And, indeed, as they watched, a set of polished silver doors slid open and Lilith Delamere came shooting out of her private lift.

Her normally cool and in-control demeanour was gone. The collar of her white shirt was awry, and her usually smooth, immaculate hair stuck out round her head like the nest of an unusually careless bird.

'SHUT IT DOWN!' she repeated shrilly. **'QUICKLY!'**

'Wait a minute!' called Maya suspiciously, her voice ringing out in the huge space. 'What do you mean, "shut it down"? That's exactly what we're here to do! I thought you were going to try and stop us!'

'Yeah,' agreed Teddy. 'Worst baddie ever! I thought the villain was supposed to give an evil chuckle and say something like, "Ah, Dream Bandits . . . I've been expecting you. Prepare to die," or something like that.'

'You don't understand!' said Lilith. 'It's not me you need to stop . . . it's *him*!'

There was a rumbling, crashing sound from behind her, and the lift doors she'd just run through were prised roughly apart. Chunks of metal door frame flew across the lab, sending sparks flying, as a gigantic leg, clad in dark pinstriped trousers, made its way through.

'Who on earth is that?' squealed Teddy, his voice

suddenly going up at least two octaves.

'That is extremely painful to sensitive cat ears,' Bin Bag complained.

'This is fascinating!' marvelled the professor. 'It seems Lilith is being pursued by her very own personal nightmare in the shape of –'

'My father!' wailed Lilith Delamere, in another dramatic moment which will also be very cool if this ever gets made into a film. In fact, it's probably the clip they'll show at the Oscars. And at that moment, Doctor Damian Delamere stepped fully into the laboratory and stood upright.

The funny thing about things that scare you is this: the more you imagine them, the larger and scarier they tend to become. And as Lilith ran from her father, he had indeed grown much larger and much, much scarier than he'd been when he was just an old oil painting. He now towered above them, as high as . . .

Sorry for the pause there, we're trying to think of a way of describing his height that doesn't use the tired old cliché of double-decker buses. It would be so, so boring to say, 'He now towered above them, as high as a double-decker bus.' We don't want to say that; it's a very dull sentence. We're trying to think of something much more original. Ah, here we go. Right.

He now towered above them, as high as twenty-four ducks standing on each other's shoulders. Oh, and also the ducks are wearing formal dress, including top hats. This isn't vital information, but we wanted you to know. Hang on, do ducks even have shoulders? Never mind, it doesn't matter. The point is, he was really, really big, OK? He was also a lot scarier than he had looked in the painting. Because he had been produced by Lilith's imagination, he had grown even as she ran away from him. His face, which had always been lined and sinister, was now twisted into a truly horrific expression of rage and hatred. His arms and legs had elongated. It was very, very scary. Forget all the stuff about ducks; we spoiled the mood there. Sorry.

'That's your dad?' Teddy gasped in fear. 'Gee, parents' evening must have been a hoot!' Maya caught sight of a fluffy tail as Bin Bag dived for cover beneath a workbench.

'This is one nightmare you can't wake up from!'

roared the giant figure of Doctor Damian Delamere, taking a swipe at Lilith with his sharp fingers and only just missing.

'Wonder how long he's been working on that one,' asked Maya drily. 'I think it's time to slow him down a bit, don't you, Bea?'

'Right,' agreed Bea, moving into position next to Maya and rolling up her sleeves. 'Let's roll.'

'On standby,' added Teddy, joining them. 'Dream Bandits . . . assemble. Been waiting to say that for weeks.'

'It kind of takes away from your cool catchphrase if you follow it up with "I've been waiting to say that for weeks",' Bea pointed out. Teddy simply shrugged.

'Right,' said Maya, regarding the enormous, terrifying figure of the imaginary Doctor Damian Delamere. 'It looks like we have a monster to fight. Any ideas?'

'We can imagine literally anything,' Bea reminded her. 'I think it's time to see how far we can take this.'

'Wonderful!' Behind them, the professor was clapping his hands in delight. 'This is going to be incredible! What strange and magnificent powers will you give yourselves, Dream Bandits? Flight? Invisibility?'

345

'Bowling balls!' cried Teddy, clicking his fingers. At once, giant brightly coloured balls began to shoot out of one hand and fly across the room. They slammed into the monster's legs, sending it reeling to one side. **'Strrrrrrrr-RIKE!'**

Teddy yelled in triumph. 'I am officially a bowling superhero!'

'Of course!' Professor Dexter told him. 'Brilliant! Yes! Don't be tied down by those boring old characters from the moving pictures! Really get your brains to work! Anything you can imagine! You keep him busy, I'll get ready to shut the machine down.' He began to make his way along the side of the laboratory.

'Army of geese!' Maya decided, attempting to click her own fingers and failing. She'd never been able to do that. But it didn't matter. Several large geese appeared beside her. **'GEESE . . . ATTACK!'**

she told them – and, honking ferociously, they obeyed.

'That's not really an army of geese,' Teddy complained. 'There are only, like, ten of them. It's just, like, a small group of geese. At best it's a cohort. You couldn't even call it a full gaggle.'

'Look, it's been a long day,' Maya explained. 'And can we please focus? That thing looks like it's got mischief on its monstrous mind.'

Lilith Delamere had plastered herself to the far wall in terror. But now that her father was distracted by the bowling balls and rampaging geese – not a sentence you hear every day – she decided to act. She made a run for the central console, shouting, 'I've got to shut it down! If I stop the machine, he'll go away!'

'He lives inside your head, Lilith!' shouted the professor in reply, though his voice was lost in the cacophony of honking and ball-bumping. 'You can't get rid of him like that! You've got to –'

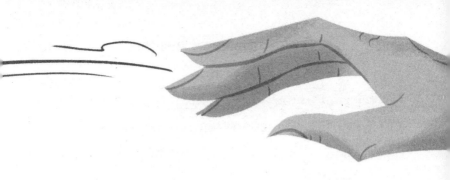

But at that moment, the enormous doctor-monster noticed Lilith dashing towards the control panel. Steadying himself on his huge legs, he batted at her with a giant hand, sending her flying across the laboratory with a scream and a puff of feathers when she briefly collided with one of the geese. (No geese were harmed in the writing of this book.)

'You were planning to broadcast this insipid nonsense into people's dreams?' roared the doctor, gesturing at one of the screens on the Clean Sleep machine, which was showing the boring dream about a crackling log fire. 'I always knew you'd come to nothing, Lilith! I always knew you didn't have the vision and ambition to run this company as well as me!'

During this display of extremely bad parenting – bad parenting which was wholly responsible for this entire mess in the first place – the injured goose was carried away on a stretcher by two of the other geese. (It's not relevant to the action, but we thought you'd want to know. It later made a full recovery and – oh, we don't know – probably went to live on a farm or something.)

'I think we can do a bit better than this rubbish!' roared Damian Delamere, bending down and plunging one finger into the main control panel of the Clean Sleep. At once, a stream of crackling electricity began to surge down his arm. The screens round the machine flickered, then began showing images of the monstrous doctor himself, his mean face leering across the room from all seven sides. 'That's better!' he snarled. 'Let's give people a proper dream, shall we? Preparing to transmit!'

'**NO!**' the professor shouted to Maya, Teddy and Bea. 'He's going to use the machine to broadcast *himself*! Everyone will be stuck in the same nightmare! We've got to stop him!' He ran forward, launching himself into a dive for the control panel, but a swat from the doctor's other huge hand sent him flying, too, in the opposite direction to Lilith. Professor Dexter landed beneath a workbench with a clatter.

'DAD!'

Maya screamed. She couldn't lose him again. She raced over, kicking chairs aside, and bent over him. The professor didn't seem badly hurt, but he was knocked out cold. Maya pushed him further underneath the bench, piling chairs in front of it to form a makeshift barrier.

'You'll be safe there,' she told her father's sleeping form, 'while we kick some giant doctor bottom.'

CHAPTER 17
LILITH DELAMERE'S NIGHTMARE

While Maya was checking on her dad, Bea and Teddy faced the enormous, imposing figure of Doctor Damian Delamere. At least, Doctor Damian Delamere as his daughter remembered him. Over the years Lilith had forgotten a lot about her father, but all the bad stuff had remained. And so the creature that had come to life from her imagination was sneering and cruel. A right nasty piece of work, not to put too fine a point on it. And now it was preparing to make itself into everybody's worst nightmare.

'Oi! Face ache!' called Teddy, hoping to distract it for at least a few minutes while someone worked out how to stop it. 'Check me out! I'm turning myself into an incredible hero that I've just thought of. Meet Spider Hands!'

In his mind, Teddy had dreamed up a wonderful character who could produce large spiders from his hands. He even had a theme song, which started, 'Spider Hands, Spider Hands, he makes spiders . . . from his hands.' But unfortunately, he didn't quite execute it correctly. To be fair, he was facing a large, frightening monster, so we can forgive him for being a bit distracted. Anyway, what actually happened was that Teddy's hands simply turned into two large spiders. It was at this point that he remembered something quite unfortunate – he was terrified of spiders.

'**ARGH!** Spider hands! **Spider hands!**'

yelled Teddy, shaking the spiders frantically to try and dislodge them. Of course, this didn't work. No matter how enthusiastically you shake your hands, they're never going to just come off. Believe us, we've tried. Teddy began to dance about, shrieking in terror, still shaking the spiders like maracas. But in fact, he did succeed in creating a slight diversion. Doctor Damian Delamere laughed cruelly.

'Oh dear,' he sneered. 'You're discovering that a little imagination can be a very dangerous thing, you poor, foolish boy.'

'You can say that again!' shouted Bea, rushing in from the other direction and imagining a giant bubble, which is actually quite hard to do while running. Have a try next time you're out for a jog. But she managed it.

'Activate the BOING bubble!'

Suddenly Bea was surrounded by a large, thick sphere. Kicking off from the floor, she flew at the doctor's face, crashing into it with an enormously satisfying noise. It's quite difficult to write down – but imagine the noise a giant bouncy bubble would make if it smashed into the face of a giant, mean doctor. Like that.

With a cry, Damian Delamere was knocked

backwards, falling away from the control panel. The jet of electricity vanished.

'**QUICK!**' shouted Maya, running across from the desk where she'd left her dad, with Bin Bag at her side. 'Stop it getting back to the machine! Imagine something!'

'Got it!' answered Teddy, who had finally managed to imagine himself a pair of normal hands again. 'Check this out . . . *It's a-MAZE-ing!*'

Suddenly, thick green hedges were erupting from the floor. Maya looked to the left and right, suddenly trapped in a long, green path with high walls of foliage on either side. 'Teddy!' she yelled. 'What did you do?'

'You can thank me later!' came Teddy's reply, deadened by the leaves. 'I put us all in a maze! He'll have to find his way through!'

'So, instead of chasing a giant monster around a large room, with clear lines of sight in all directions,' came Bea's voice from somewhere ahead, 'we are now trapped in a large maze, being chased by a monster that is so tall, it can probably step right over these hedges.'

'Oh yeah,' Teddy replied. 'I'll make them higher!'

'Teddy, no!' Maya shouted. But it was too late. With a creaking and rustling, the hedges expanded upward until they almost reached the ceiling.

'There you go!' said Teddy, though his voice now sounded faint and far away. 'Right – which way to the machine? Then we can get it turned off.'

'It's your maze!' shouted Bea. 'Don't you know the way?'

'If I knew the way,' Teddy explained patiently, 'it wouldn't be a maze, would it? It would just be a load of decorative shrubbery. The very definition

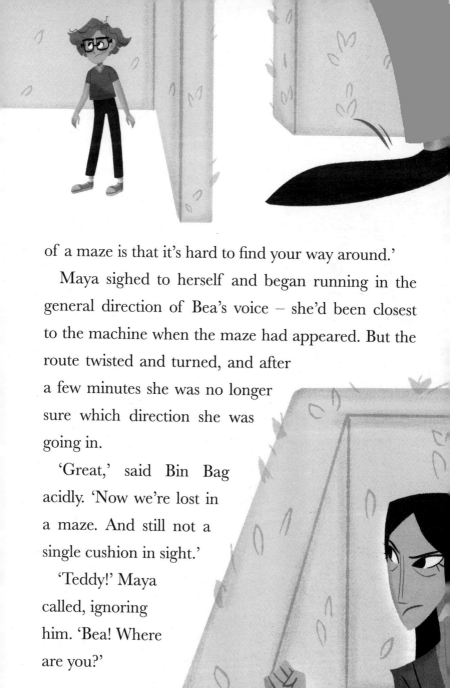

of a maze is that it's hard to find your way around.'

Maya sighed to herself and began running in the general direction of Bea's voice – she'd been closest to the machine when the maze had appeared. But the route twisted and turned, and after a few minutes she was no longer sure which direction she was going in.

'Great,' said Bin Bag acidly. 'Now we're lost in a maze. And still not a single cushion in sight.'

'Teddy!' Maya called, ignoring him. 'Bea! Where are you?'

'Maya?' she heard a faint reply. 'Over here!' But the voice echoed so strangely through the tall walls of foliage, it was impossible to tell exactly where it came from.

'If you can hear me, Teddy,' she shouted as loudly as she could as she ran, 'you've got to get rid of this maze! We're never going to find that creature before it –'

Maya stopped dead as she rounded a corner and almost ran smack into Lilith Delamere, who was dashing in the other direction. The two of them regarded each other suspiciously.

'I don't know what you're looking at me like that for,' said Lilith haughtily.

'Imprisoning my dad in a nightmare deserved this look on its own,' said Maya heatedly. 'But that's not all you did, is it? You also visited him in hospital, pretending to be worried about him, when in fact you were just checking he was out of action. You used your weird private army to spy on me and my mum. You used my dad's invention to make a scary machine, with which you planned to steal everyone's dreams and replace them with adverts. And now you've created some mad imaginary version of your evil dad, who's about to use your stupid creation to insert himself into everybody's nightmares. That's –' she had been ticking the evil things off on her fingers as she went – 'at least five reasons to look at you *like that*. You deserve a lot more than just a look, missy.' Maya's mum always called her missy when she was telling her off, and it just slipped out, but it kind of worked.

Lilith looked slightly shamefaced at this angry plot summary. 'Yes, well . . .' she hedged, shuffling her feet and looking over her shoulder along the long, green tunnel. 'But now you can see what was in my dreams . . . perhaps you can understand why I wanted to stop them.'

'You have no right to stop other people's dreams, though!' yelled Maya, losing her temper. 'Just because you have nightmares, it doesn't give you the right to take other people's dreams away!

NOBODY has that right!'

Lilith licked her thin lips, her eyes downcast, and looked as if she were about to reply. But then her face blanched. With a tearing sound, the enormous figure of Doctor Damian Delamere burst through the wall of the maze and faced them, smashing a bony fist into his palm. 'There you are, you sad disappointment!' he bellowed, taking a threatening step forward. Without thinking, Maya and Lilith turned tail together and ran.

As they fled, Maya's brain was working overtime. She realized for the first time that she actually felt a little sorry for Lilith. If this was the father she'd produced out of her imagination – that was pretty tragic. Maya thought about her own kindly dad, and her eyes tickled with regret that Lilith didn't have that relationship with her own father. But there was no time to say anything. It's an awkward conversation to start at the best of times – let alone when you're being chased around a maze by a huge monster.

Maya led Lilith, who was sobbing with fright, round corners and down long green hallways – the stamping feet of the giant doctor never far behind. And as they went, the whole scene started to feel more than a little familiar.

'This feels more than a little familiar,' confirmed

Bin Bag – seeming to read her thoughts, which was unsurprising, considering he was one of them.

'I know.' Maya panted, glancing down at him. 'It's like –'

'The nightmare where your dad was trapped,' Bin Bag concluded. Maya nodded, thinking hard. It was the feeling of being chased that had brought it home to her – that tingling in your legs and the shiver on the back of your neck.

'Lilith!' she said suddenly. 'I've just realized something!'

'It'll have to wait!' snapped Lilith. Her hair and eyes were wild, and she looked completely deranged.

Maya realized she needed a moment to try and calm her down – she was no use at all in this state. Concentrating briefly, she tried to imagine a safe haven where they could hide out, if only for a few moments, so she could talk to Lilith. Somewhere nothing bad could happen to her. She didn't have to think for long. With a **popping** and a **creaking** of planks, a long, low wooden building materialized in front of them and she quickly led them inside.

'What on earth is this?' said Lilith frantically, looking around at the cluttered workbench, the white wall covered in doodles and the neon sign reading

'It's my dad's workshop from the bottom of our garden,' Maya told her, immediately feeling a little more at ease as the door swung shut behind them.

'Now, this is more like it,' said Bin Bag, immediately jumping up on to the bench and seeking out a pile of papers to settle down on.

Maya smiled, but immediately collected herself. This might be her favourite place in the whole world, but that wouldn't keep the monstrous doctor out. 'Lilith, listen,' she said quickly. 'We don't have long. There's only one way to stop that thing out there, and you've got to do it. You need to trust me.'

There was a loud

BOOM,

and the shed door quaked on its hinges. Specks of dust dropped from the ceiling as the wooden walls shook. 'He's breaking in!' wailed Lilith. 'We're trapped in here, you stupid girl! Trapped!'

'Little pigs, little pigs . . .' bellowed the voice of Lilith's father. 'Let me come in . . .'

'That is downright creepy,' said Maya, as an aside. 'Now, Lilith, listen. That monster out there is not your dad.'

'It is!' wailed Lilith. 'He came out of the picture! It's got his name underneath and everything!'

'No!' insisted Maya. 'This is your nightmare, and that . . . that monster is something you created. It's your own twisted memory of your dad. But you know what my own dad told me once?'

'What?' said Lilith tensely, wiping one of the dusty windows to look outside.

'If there's a monster in your dreams,' said Maya, 'chances are it's got something to tell you. Or there's something *you* need to tell *it.*'

'Well, I know what he wants to tell me,' Lilith replied glumly. 'He tells me every time I fall asleep. He tells me I'm useless and a disappointment, and he wishes he hadn't been forced to leave his laboratory to me.'

'And what do you want to say back?' said Maya.

'What?' Lilith looked dumbfounded by the question.

'I said –' Maya planted her feet firmly apart and her hands on her hips – 'what do you want to say back to him? Is he right? *Are* you useless?'

'Well, of course I'm not!' said Lilith hotly, turning away from the window. 'I'm in charge of one of the foremost sleep-science laboratories on the planet! I've made a massive success of it!'

'Well, don't tell me,' said Maya gently, gesturing towards the door. 'Tell him. Because I was in a nightmare once before, and do you know what I discovered?'

'What?' asked Lilith uncertainly.

'That if you're being chased, and you keep running away, you just end up going in circles,' Maya Clayton told her, glancing over at Bin Bag, who nodded encouragingly. 'If you want to get where you need to go, you need to turn the tables.'

'And what does that mean?' Lilith asked.

'It means,' Maya replied, 'that you've been frightened

of dreaming about your dad for too long. You can't run away from him for ever, you know. He's inside your head. **It's time for YOU to chase HIM instead.** That's the only way to properly get rid of him.'

Lilith Delamere regarded Maya with a strange expression. She looked rather frightened, but then her face seemed to soften as she let out a long, shuddering sigh. Clenching her fists, she rose to her feet.

Outside in the maze, Doctor Damian Delamere had just lifted up one of his enormous, polished shoes, preparing to stomp down on the garden shed with horrifying force. But before he could strike, the shed door flew open and the figure of Lilith Delamere appeared, shaking with suppressed rage.

'I am not useless!' she yelled at the top of her voice. 'And you are nothing but a mean, bitter old man!'

The doctor hesitated, one foot still suspended in mid-air.

'I have made this laboratory better than you could ever have dreamed,' Lilith continued, shaking an angry finger, 'with hard work and, yes, with talent! I am talented! And I am sick to death of you hanging behind my chair, silently disapproving of everything I do! What do you know, anyway?'

Maya came to the doorway behind Lilith. She watched this bizarre scene unfold and felt strangely invested in Lilith's battle. 'I think it's working,' she whispered encouragingly, as the giant doctor lowered his leg and took an uncertain step backwards.

But Lilith Delamere didn't need any encouragement. It was as if a dam inside her had burst. 'Would it have killed you to say you were proud of me?' she shrieked, advancing on the monster, which was now backing away, and, Maya realized, growing gradually smaller. 'Don't you *dare* run away from me,' scolded Lilith. 'I'm only just getting started! You've got a lot of explaining to do, you . . .

. . . *you mouldy old TOAD!*'

'Mouldy old toad?' Maya repeated to herself, shrugging. 'Oh, well, whatever works, I suppose.' And it certainly did work. The doctor turned tail and began running away through the maze, Lilith dashing after him, still flinging home truths at his retreating back like grenades. Maya dashed off in pursuit.

'What about the nice comfortable shed?' wailed Bin Bag from the doorway. 'Aren't we staying in the shed? Well, apparently not,' he huffed, jogging to catch up with Maya.

Once or twice Maya lost the pair of them as they turned corners, but every time she caught up she was heartened to see that the doctor was growing smaller and smaller and less scary with every lash of Lilith's tongue.

'Get back in your stupid old picture, you mangy goat!' she was yelling. 'This is my company now! You've got no business criticizing! Wind your wrinkly old neck in!'

'Sounds like quite a therapy session going on there,' came a voice from

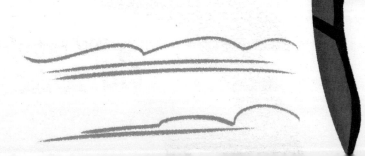

Maya's right. Teddy was approaching down another of the maze's narrow green avenues. 'Lilith had a few issues with her old dad to work out, eh?' he continued.

'Will you *please* get rid of this stupid maze you've imagined?' panted Maya in reply.

'Oh, right,' said Teddy. 'Sorry, I thought you liked it.'

'Well, I don't. No one likes mazes, not after the first five minutes, anyway.'

'Fair enough.' Teddy shrugged, screwing up his face briefly. At once, the enormous hedges began to shrink downwards like a clever time-lapse film being screened backwards. They curled back into the ground, leaving the huge room open and empty once more. It seemed even more huge than before, the tower of the Clean Sleep now once again visible in the middle, with a few strands of green foliage stuck to it here and there. And ahead of them were the figures of Lilith Delamere and her father.

Although Doctor Damian Delamere was smaller and less monstrous than before, he was still apparently a thoroughly nasty piece of work. Maya clearly saw his expression change as the hedges receded like a green tide and he caught sight of the tower of machinery. Immediately his expression of fear was replaced by one of cunning, and he made a desperate dash towards the control panel.

'He's still trying to send out nightmares!' Maya cried in desperation. 'We've got to stop him!'

'Bowling balls again?' queried Teddy.

'How about geese?' asked Bea, running out from behind the Clean Sleep.

'It's got to be Lilith!' Maya realized. 'He's her nightmare – she's the only one who can get rid of him. Lilith!' she yelled. 'Keep going! You've almost got him! But you mustn't let him reach the machine!

He'll become EVERYONE'S NIGHTMARE if he does!'

Lilith Delamere had briefly stopped her rant when the maze melted away. But hearing Maya's shout, she started after the monstrous version of her father once again. 'Don't you dare try and take over my laboratory, you sour-faced . . . halibut.'

Unable to stop herself, Maya burst into peals of

laughter. 'Halibut?' she hooted. Teddy and Bea, she could see, were laughing too.

Lilith smiled, a little reluctantly. 'Well, look at him –' She gestured towards the running figure. 'He does look like a stupid old halibut, doesn't he? A nasty, smelly halibut wearing a suit.'

As she spoke, her face twitched oddly. And then Lilith Delamere did something she hadn't done for several years. First a slight smile appeared on her face. Then she chuckled.

'Are you smiling?' asked Maya, wiping her eyes. 'You are, aren't you? You're smiling at the thought of your dad being a fish in a suit.'

'There is something kind of cod-esque about him, come to think of it,' Teddy added.

Lilith's smile grew even wider, like a small crack in a dam. And then, all at once, the dam burst. And she exploded into huge convulsions of joyous laughter. **'COD MAN!'** she sputtered, pointing at the fleeing doctor with a shaking finger.

'Silly old HADDOCK!'

And the waves of laughter slammed into the back of Doctor Damian Delamere, shrinking him even further. Even as he made a final, desperate dash for the control panel, he shrivelled and curled in on himself, finally disappearing with a wet, fishy, slapping noise.

'Where's he gone?' asked Teddy, walking over and examining the floor.

'Back in his painting, where he belongs,' said Lilith, coming over to join him and dusting her hands together.

'I'm not sure,' said Maya, grinning at Teddy, 'but I think the Dream Bandits just saved the day.'

'We did save the day, didn't we?' replied Teddy, as Bea rushed over and grabbed them both in a group hug. 'I've always wanted to do that. Cool.'

They all turned their heads at a scraping of chairs from the other side of the laboratory. 'What did I miss?' asked a dazed Professor Dexter, levering himself out from beneath the workbench.

'What did I miss?' came another voice from the doorway at exactly the same time. Doctor Julia Flamewood rushed in, looking hot and bothered.

'You're a bit late for the climactic battle scene, Mum,' Teddy scolded her.

'I've been held up in reception,' Julia apologized. 'That unicorn insisted on performing a medley of show tunes before it would let me through. I had to watch the whole thing. And, several times, join in with the chorus.'

'What you both missed,' Lilith replied, 'is Maya saving me – by giving me some truly excellent advice.'

'Are you smiling again?' Maya asked suspiciously.

'She definitely is smiling,' confirmed Bin Bag, gazing up at Lilith with his large green eyes.

'Don't worry,' said Lilith, 'I'll try not to make a habit of it.'

'What was the advice?' the professor asked, pushing

more chairs out of the way and walking over to join them.

'Oh, just something you told me once,' said Maya airily. 'The old "not running away from monsters" trick, you might call it.' He squeezed her shoulder in pride.

'Anyone else think we need to turn off this scary machine before something else tries to rob everyone's dreams?' asked Bea, looking up at the gleaming metal tower.

'I think that's an excellent idea,' agreed Lilith. 'And I think it should be Maya.' She held out a hand, indicating a large switch beside the main control panel.

'It seems a shame,' said Maya. 'You'll lose the jungle in your reception area. And the unicorn. And the seal phone.'

'Oh, not permanently, I hope,' Lilith said with a grin. 'There are going to be a few changes around here. I think there's a lot about dreams I still need to find out. With your father's help, hopefully. Maybe we won't keep the jungle, but we'll certainly add a bit more colour to this place.'

'But for now,' Professor Dexter went on, 'I think Bea's right. We need to shut this down.'

Maya nodded and placed a hand on the switch. Bin Bag leaped up on to the console and nuzzled against her. 'Wait a minute,' she said, 'you're about to disappear too!'

'I live inside your head, silly human,' Bin Bag replied. 'But it's been nice to come out and have a proper run about, I must say.'

'Thanks for everything,' Maya told him seriously.

'No, no, thank you,' replied the cat as Maya brushed away a small tear and, before she had time to change her mind, decisively threw the switch downwards.

'See you tonight,' said Bin Bag as he vanished.

CHAPTER 18
TWO WEEKS LATER...

'Tea's up, Scribbles!' Professor Dexter pushed his way through the door of his workshop to find Maya and her mum both sitting crossed-legged in front of the Doodle Wall. 'What are you both up to?' he asked, setting down a tray full of steaming mugs.

'Oh, just a few drawings from the last few weeks,' replied Maya's mum, pen in hand.

'Yeah, just boring, real-life stuff, you know,' confirmed Maya. On the white wall in front of her she had drawn a unicorn holding a microphone, performing to a crowd of llamas, which her mum was now colouring in.

'That's an excellent likeness of Donald,' her father congratulated her, wandering over to ruffle her hair.

'He certainly does love that hokey-cokey.'

'It's called karaoke, Dad,' said Maya with a grin.

'Ah, yes, of course.' The professor grinned. 'He looks like he might be rather chilly, though. How about giving him a scarf like mine?' He threw the end of his Thinking Scarf over one shoulder.

'Great idea!' Sticking out her tongue in concentration, Maya began to add a stripy scarf to her picture.

'Thanks for the tea,' said her mum, abandoning her llama colouring to grab a mug. 'Oooh, and biscuits! Excellent!' She pushed a chocolate digestive into her mouth and munched contentedly while Maya continued her drawing. 'Who'd have thought your daydreaming would be so useful, eh?' she mused through a mouthful of crumbs. 'I'll never tell you off for being in a world of your own again, that's for sure! Not now I know what an amazing world it is.'

'They'll be here any minute,' said Professor Dexter, peering out of the window. And then, as the toot of a horn sounded on the road outside, 'Ah! Right on time.'

The sound of voices came down the path beside the house, and after a few seconds the garden filled with

Flamewoods. Teddy and Bea led the way, followed by Mr Flamewood bearing a large brown-paper parcel. Doctor Julia Flamewood came last, looking around slightly tentatively, but she visibly relaxed when the professor threw open the workshop door with a cry of welcome.

'Come in! Come in! There is tea! There are biscuits!'

Soon the wooden shed was rammed with people and excited chatter. Maya scrambled up from the floor, putting her pens away just in time before she was enveloped in a huge hug from Bea. Matt Flamewood was presenting Maya's mum with the brown-paper package, exclaiming, 'Brought a few new pillows for you, Mrs Clayton! Made, of course, from the finest –'

'Flamewood Floaty Foam!' chorused Maya and her mum, catching each other's eye and grinning.

Soon, everyone had managed to find a cup and somewhere to sit. The professor swept piles of paper from the ragged old sofa to make space for Matt and Julia, who sat close together, holding hands.

'Well, it's been a funny few weeks,' Julia began

nervously, blushing. 'I must say, Dexter, that I'm so sorry . . .'

'Think no more of it,' the professor told her seriously. 'You were given no choice. I think what's most important is that we thank our rescuers.' Lifting his mug in a toast, he beamed around at Maya, Teddy and Bea.

'To the **DREAM BANDITS!**'

'To the Dream Bandits!' the other adults echoed, chinking their tea together in celebration.

'Turns out I have a couple of very sneaky children!' laughed Julia nervously. 'To be able to recreate our research, Dexter! Contact Maya without anyone realizing . . .'

'Storm a hospital . . .' continued the professor, his eyes twinkling.

'Invade the dreams of Somnia's head of security and give him a fear of cows,' added Tess, who had now been brought up to speed with the whole plot.

'And save bedtime for everyone!' completed Matt, patting the pillows on the sofa beside him.

'Sounds pretty impressive, when you put it like that,' said Teddy, looking uncharacteristically embarrassed. 'You make us sound like, I dunno . . .'

'Spies? Secret agents?' suggested Bea.

'Like a pretty impressive team,' Teddy corrected, cuffing her affectionately on the shoulder.

'And you won't believe what Somnia looks like now!' added Julia excitedly. 'Lilith's completely . . . well, you're about to see for yourselves.'

'Shall we?' invited the professor, getting to his feet.

The Flamewoods' van was parked on the street outside, and Maya was surprised to see that the back was crammed with more large packages. 'Matt's just been given a big contract from Lilith to supply soft furnishings for the Heptagon!' explained Julia.

'And you'll never guess what she's ordered for her own bed at home,' said Matt. 'Only my bounciest creation yet – a little invention I like to call Matt's Marvellous Mega Mattress! It's massive! She says she's been doing so much sleeping, she wants to do it in style! And there's no style like Flamewood style,' he added, doing finger guns as the twins silently cringed behind him.

'Soft furnishings in the Heptagon?' queried Maya. 'I didn't think there was anything soft in that entire building.'

'Well, like I said, things have changed,' Julia told her. 'This is the first consignment of beanbags for the new break rooms.'

'Lilith Delamere never really struck me as a bean-baggy sort of a person,' murmured Maya, half to herself, as she found a space among the squashy packages and settled down. But as she was about to discover, things at Somnia Incorporated had indeed changed.

*

'Welcome to the Heptagon . . . headquarters of Somnia Incorporated,' said Lilith's Delamere's voice as the automatic glass doors slid smoothly open. Maya led the way inside, to see the real-life Lilith approaching across reception. At least, she was fairly sure it was Lilith – she had to look very closely before she was positive.

The bags under Lilith's eyes had gone. In fact, now that she was able to enjoy a proper night's sleep, without dreams of her father terrifying her, she looked completely different, as if someone had turned up the brightness on her like a computer screen.

'Well, if it isn't the Dream Bandits,' she said to Teddy, Bea and Maya. 'Welcome to the new Somnia!'

'And have a dreamy day!' added a voice from behind her. The unicorn trotted into view, looking very spick and span, with its tail and mane neatly combed.

'Morning, Donald,' said Lilith.

'And good morning to you, Lil. Luuurve the outfit, by the way,' the unicorn told her, rearing up slightly so it could do jazz hooves with its front legs. 'It's fab-u-licious! You're giving me a run for my money, honey – and I'm mythical! That red really makes your eyes pop!'

Lilith was wearing a bright red dress. And yes, clever clogs, well remembered:

it was the very same dress that she'd worn on her first day at work all those years ago, which her father had hated so much. It had been sitting in her wardrobe since then, and probably would have been feeling pretty hard done by if dresses had feelings. But today, if dresses could feel happy, it would have been on top of the world. Even though it was, in fact, on top of Lilith.

'Thank you, Donald.' Lilith smiled. Yes, we said 'smiled' – it's not a misprint. She'd been doing a lot more smiling over the last two weeks. 'Everything running according to plan?' she asked the unicorn.

'Oh no, Ms Delamere,' he responded with a smirk. 'Not in the least. The llamas are going bananas on the fourth floor. The pirate ship has run aground in the ball pit, and all the toilets in the building are full of lime-flavoured jelly instead of water. It's total, if rather tasty, chaos.'

'Excellent,' she replied with an answering grin. 'Carry on.' The unicorn saluted smartly and trotted back towards the reception desk.

'So, things have changed around here a little bit,' breathed an awestruck Teddy, scanning the reception area, which looked very slightly different from a fortnight ago. Well, quite a lot different, actually. Wholly different. Different-a-rama, we might almost say – though we probably won't; it sounds stupid.

The hard chairs and the boring white walls were gone. Instead there was bright paintwork, tall plants and cactuses (oh, all right, cacti) scattered among comfortable, squashy armchairs in shades of blue, mustard and red. And above the reception desk was the most striking new addition – an enormous map of the world, lit up in the centre to indicate where it was daytime. And here and there across the massive map, concentrated most strongly in the dark areas, were countless tiny bursts of colour, like flowers or miniature explosions of vibrant, brightly hued powder.

'This is amazing!' said Maya.

'Slightly garish for my taste,' said a voice from low down beside her. Maya looked down to see that Bin

Bag had popped back into existence beside her.

'So the Dream Field's back?' asked Maya, amazed.

'Told you there had been some changes,' her father said, walking over to stand beside Lilith.

'The Dream Field is indeed back,' she told Maya. 'We've permanently meshed the building with the field, so we can experience dreams from all over the world.' She indicated the huge map above the reception desk. 'That's a running tally of all the dreams being experienced across the planet.'

'I can see some where it's daylight,' said Maya, staring up at the map.

'Siesta time,' explained the professor. 'Or just a good old-fashioned afternoon nap, if you prefer. I always get wonderful dreams after a really great lunch.'

'So . . . no plans to replace dreams with your own versions any more, then?' asked Bin Bag. Maya had wanted to ask the question herself but had felt it slightly impolite – obviously the cat-like part of her brain felt differently.

Lilith looked slightly embarrassed. 'No,' she said slowly. 'And I have to thank you for explaining that to me so clearly. I'd been running away for a long time, you see. Running away from my memory of my father and what he thought of me. It was you who told me to turn round, and, well . . . Come and see.'

Together they all walked over to a set of doors, which opened ahead of them.

'I'm just popping to the bathroom, if that's OK, Ms Delamere,' said the unicorn as they passed.

'Yes, Donald, that's fine,' said Lilith. 'But what are you taking a spoon with you for?'

'Er, nothing,' said the unicorn, looking sheepish and attempting to hide the spoon behind its back. 'Definitely not for toilet jelly.'

'If you want jelly, there's jelly in the break room,' Lilith told him. The unicorn nodded reluctantly and trotted off.

'Break room? Toilet jelly?' queried Maya. 'Things really are running a bit differently around here.'

'Oh yes,' agreed Lilith, indicating the doors to the right and left as they walked down the brightly painted passageway, which was lined with colourful pictures. Instead of having boring, office-like names, the rooms were now labelled things like BUS DOG (dog driving a bus), MEGA BOING: NO SHOES (giant trampoline) and RAINFOREST WATER PARK.

'This place is completely batty,' decided Bin Bag.

'I certainly hope so,' Lilith replied. 'And coming from a talking cat, I'll take that as a huge compliment.'

'*Touché*,' Bin Bag agreed in a flawless French accent.

'I like the pictures,' Bea piped up. 'Hopefully none of them are going to come to life and start chasing us this time, though.'

'No,' laughed Lilith. 'Well, hopefully not.'

'We're not expecting a visit from your dad, then,' asked Teddy, just wanting to make sure.

'Oh, him,' said Lilith dismissively. 'No, no. You know the store cupboard on the fourth floor, Dexter? The one where we keep all the spare light bulbs and the cleaning supplies?'

'Er, I believe so, yes,' said the professor, who was ambling along beside her.

'I've hung him in there, to keep the mops company. There was a horrible damp patch on the wall and I needed something to cover it up. He was just the right

size and, do you know,
I feel so much better not
having him looking over my shoulder all
the time.'

'I'm sure he can't have been quite as mean in real life
as you imagined him,' said Maya kindly.

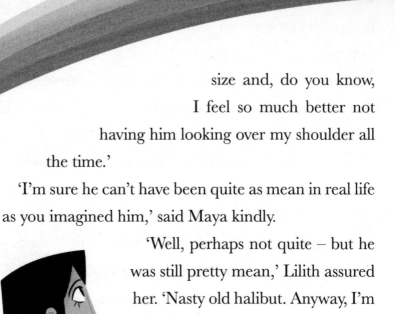

'Well, perhaps not quite – but he
was still pretty mean,' Lilith assured
her. 'Nasty old halibut. Anyway, I'm
sure he's having a lovely time in the
cupboard.'

When they reached the central
laboratory, Maya, remembering the

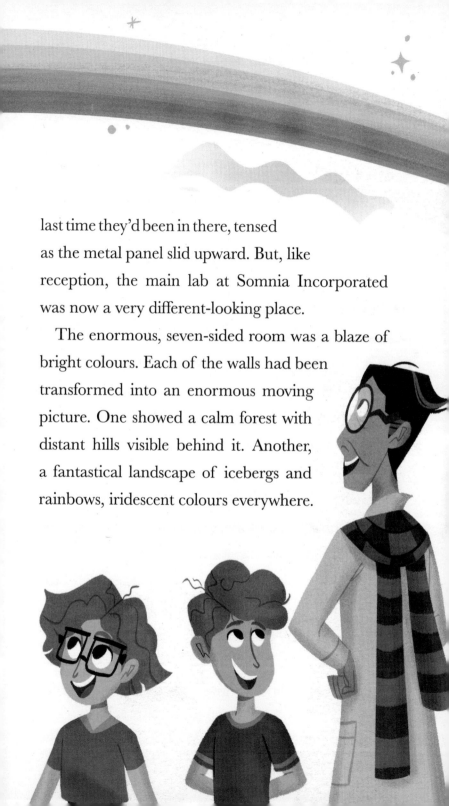

last time they'd been in there, tensed
as the metal panel slid upward. But, like
reception, the main lab at Somnia Incorporated
was now a very different-looking place.

The enormous, seven-sided room was a blaze of
bright colours. Each of the walls had been
transformed into an enormous moving
picture. One showed a calm forest with
distant hills visible behind it. Another,
a fantastical landscape of icebergs and
rainbows, iridescent colours everywhere.

'Whoa!' said Maya, Teddy and Bea at exactly the same time.

'Yes, it is rather *whoa*, isn't it?' said Lilith, grinning. 'All inspired by your father, Maya. And, of course, by you!'

'Me?'

'Yes.' Lilith smiled once again – it was in danger of becoming a habit. 'I saw your Doodle Wall when you imagined your father's workshop. And I wanted to answer that very important question –' She pointed up at a huge sign, so high that Maya hadn't noticed it. WHAT IF? it read.

'It is impressive,' said Bin Bag grudgingly. 'Though it does all look rather exhausting.' He wandered over to a nearby desk and curled up underneath it.

'So, what do you think?' asked Professor Dexter, extending his arms and spinning round to show off the room, scarf flapping.

'It's a giant version of the Zoetrope!' marvelled Bea.

'I knew you'd get it straight away,' he congratulated her. Maya gave her friend's arm a little squeeze.

'We're able to explore dreams like never before,' Lilith told them. 'And it's giving us countless ideas for inventions, solutions to problems . . .'

'So, you're looking into people's dreams and stealing their ideas?' questioned Maya. 'Are you sure that isn't just the tiniest bit . . . well, evil?'

'I'm keeping a close eye on her,' her father promised. 'Anything she actually invents, we'll make sure the dreamer gets the credit.'

'Besides,' added Lilith, 'everything we've found so far has been completely useless!'

'Useless?' Bea queried.

'Oh yes,' Lilith told her. 'Jelly in the toilet. Dog driving a bus. No practical use whatsoever. But, you see, the main thing is . . .

I'm having such tremendous FUN!'

'Paperclips, anyone?' came a reedy voice from behind them. They all turned to see General Pheare in the doorway, dressed in a set of brown overalls and pushing a trolley. 'Notepads?' he went on. 'Hole punch? Staples?'

'You remember Mr Pheare, of course?' said Lilith airily. 'I've put him in charge of stationery. Unfortunately my father gave him a cast-iron contract, so I can't fire him, but I found him a job where he can't do too much mischief. No, thank you, General,' she said loudly. 'No office supplies here, thank you.'

'She says she doesn't need any office supplies, sir!' said a voice, and Private Hancock appeared in the doorway beside Pheare, also dressed in overalls.

'Yes, I can hear perfectly well, thank you, Hancock,' said Pheare gruffly. He came to attention and saluted. 'Very well, sir. I shall see if any supplies are needed elsewhere.' He turned and pushed the trolley out of sight, piping, 'Pencils! Rubbers! Lamination pouches!' as if he were desperately trying to sell ice creams on the beach before they all melted.

'I haven't got the heart to tell him the whole office is completely paperless,' said Lilith, grinning. 'Anyway, it keeps him busy.'

At that moment, there was a commotion on the far side of the lab. The huge wall, which was showing an enormous mountain range, rippled, and a llama came bursting out.

'LLAMERGENCY!'

it cried, so loudly that it woke up Bin Bag underneath the desk.

'Scared the life out of me,' he said with a huff, turning round a couple of times and lying back down again.

They all rushed over. 'Whatever is the matter, Jeff?' asked Lilith in concern.

'Our bananas have been stolen!' squeaked the llama dramatically **'It's a LLAMA DISASTER!'**

Teddy, Maya and Bea were exchanging glances. 'Are you thinking what I'm thinking?' Teddy asked.

'Are you thinking, *This sounds like a job for the Dream Bandits?*' replied Maya.

'I am absolutely thinking that,' he confirmed.

'In that case, yes,' said Maya. 'I am indeed thinking what you're thinking.'

'Bea,' Teddy began, 'are you thinking –'

'Yes!' she interrupted him. 'Shall we just get on with it?'

Maya looked across at Professor Dexter. 'Can we, Dad?' she asked. In reply, he gave a slight bow and extended his hand as if to say, 'Be my guest.'

'In that case,' said Maya Clayton, 'Dream Bandits, assemble!'

'Not forgetting your noble steed!' added Donald the unicorn, galloping up, still licking jelly from around his mouth. 'Climb aboard!'

The three of them clambered on to his back.

'Giddy up, Donald!' cried Maya. 'Ride like the wind! Hyaaa!'

The unicorn reared and gave a loud, dramatic neigh before charging towards the shimmering picture in front of them. Lilith Delamere and Professor Dexter watched as the unicorn vanished into the dream, leaving only a few ripples behind, while a distant shout of

'Let's go save those BANANAS!'

was carried faintly back towards them on the breeze.

THE END

ACKNOWLEDGEMENTS

Gregstopher and Chrisophery would like to acknowledge the following people for being brilliant. We'd like to call this section 'Acknowledgements'.

FROM GREG: Firstly, my dear friend, Chris. We did it. Again! Your humour and intelligence never ceases to amaze me and I love how our brains work together.

Thank you to Steph for taking us on as acorns – we hope one day to become sturdy oaks for you to swing on. (I'll stop the analogy there before it gets weirder.)

To Carmen and the rest of the Puffins, thank you for making us feel so welcome. It's unbearably exciting to be published by such a place. Here's to many more adventures (contractually at least two more).

Thank you as ever to Mum and Dad for giving me

books and reading to me. It was a very good idea.

And finally, to Bella, for keeping me full of laughter, love and light when the world seemed so sad, unkind and dark. I love you.

FROM CHRIS: Greg, thanks so much for the thanks in your section of these acknowledgements. It's a pleasure writing this part of the aforementioned acknowledgements next to such kind words and may I just add: back atcha. What shall we do next?

To Stephanie: you are a flipping machine and we love you dearly. Never stop being so very, very Stephanie.

To the Chief Puffin and her many Puffinions, I would also like to add: Kark! Which is puffin language for 'Thanks, you're amazing'.

Thanks to Jenny and Lucas for constantly thrashing me at table tennis and much more besides.

And finally, to Mabel the cat: Not every time I go to the fridge is to get something for you, OK? Maybe if I write this in an actual book you'll take it in.

CHRIS SMITH has wanted to be an author ever since he was eight and won a competition by writing a story about a baby dinosaur who loved biscuits. That story is soon to be brought to life as a blockbuster Hollywood movie. Not really, he made that part up. Chris worked for many years as a newsreader and presenter on radio stations including Xfm and BBC Radio 1. That's where he met Greg James, and in between messing about on the airwaves the pair created the bestselling Kid Normal series. Chris lives in north London with his family and a cat called Mabel who can turn invisible.
@itschrissmith

GREG JAMES hasn't yet won a story writing competition but hopes that it will happen one day. Maybe even with this new book you've just read. As well as writing the aforementioned bestselling Kid Normal series with Chris Smith, Greg is the host of *The Radio 1 Breakfast Show*, the loosely cricket-based podcast *Tailenders* and Radio 4's *Rewinder*. Basically he's turned all his favourite things into work and now has no hobbies. Greg also lives in north London but with his own family. This includes his wife, Bella, and his dog, Barney, who is staring at him impatiently because he wants to go for a walk.

@gregjames

HI THERE!

Did you enjoy *The Great Dream Robbery*? Those were some pretty epic dreams, weren't they? Are your dreams as fantastic and full of action packed adventures as Maya and the Dream Bandits's ?

Well, this is your chance to tell us all about them in your very own dream journal – just like the one Teddy and Bea use.

Turn the page to fill in the journal with all your weird and wonderful dreams, or you could even write your very own story about dreams featuring the characters! Maybe avoid Lilith's dad though – he's a bit of a nightmare really, isn't he?

Yours dreamily,

Greg and **Chris**

...................................'S DREAM JOURNAL